A Collection of Short Stories for Young Adults

By M. L. Stimpson

Special thanks to the Job Corps of Cleveland –
this one's for you!

Table of Contents

First and Last Wish

Vocabulary Guide – "First and Last Wish"

Words (in order of appearance)	Definition	Example Sentence
Clamor (v)	Gather around and make a fuss; raise an outcry	The clamor of children made it hard to hear what Santa Claus had to say.
Bogus	Fake; false	She tried to get into the club with a bogus I.D.
Series	Several actions or events happening one right after the other	After a series of colds and infections, they discovered that her immune system had been compromised.
Refrain	Not do something you wish to do	She had to refrain from eating candy after being diagnosed with diabetes.
Absurd	Completely silly or unreasonable	It seems absurd to wait three days to see a film that only lasts 90 minutes.
Array	A group of things or people	He presented her with a beautiful array of flowers.
assert	To behave aggressively; to strongly state your rights	In the 1920's, women began to assert themselves politically.

Before Reading Questions – "First and Last Wish"
1. Do you think some people are just unlucky?
2. Can someone who has been to prison for a long time ever be trusted again?
3. Do you think that going to jail or prison changes a person?
4. Is it ever okay to decide not to help a family member?

All Daniel Bailey knew about his father was that the man had been in prison since the month before Daniel was born, twenty years ago. Once a year, Daniel's mother forced him to visit his paternal relatives. "Do I have to go?" he nearly whined. The whole routine was rather lame, not to mention the fact that the Baileys didn't seem to care one way or the other about Daniel. Though he still lived in the same town where his father's side of the family resided, none of the Baileys ever made the trip to Daniel's house to check on him.

As always, Daniel's mother insisted. "No matter what happened with your father, you still need to know your family. You don't want to fall in love with some girl and find out she's your cousin, do you?"

"That's sick, Mom."

Annie laughed as she ordered Daniel to help his younger brother, Jordan, finish buttoning his coat.

"Why do I have to go, Mom? He's not *my* dad," Jordan announced his dismay for the first time.

"See what you've done? Now your brother is complaining," Annie fussed. She pushed her bangs behind both ears and bent down to address Jordan's grievance. "You're going because I said so."

The trio made the short drive to Grandmother Bailey's trailer for their annual holiday visit. Every year, the same thing happened.

"Oh, Daniel," Grandma Bailey would exclaim, "you're the spitting image of your father when he was your age! Come here. Let me get a look at you." Grandma Bailey pulled Daniel into a hug while plopping a sloppy, spitty kiss on his cheek. For the past four years, she had pulled Jordan in for a wet one, too.

Finally, she hugged Annie and lamented, "You're the best daughter-in-law I never had," between coughing spells.

"Oh, I'm sure you say that to all of Levi's old girlfriends," Annie repeated her line as well.

This time was no different. The small family room filled with relatives who clamored over Daniel first, Jordan second, and finally Annie. There was always good food and always some small talk of how well Annie was doing raising the boys alone. Now that Daniel was twenty and had earned his pharmacy technician certification from the Cleveland Job Corps, gotten a good job, and moved into his own apartment, he was living proof that Annie had done well despite the hardships of single motherhood.

But soon, the conversation worked its way around to material things in what Daniel now recognized as "the hateration conversation." Someone looked out the window to see what kind of car Annie was driving and then reported it to the room. "Wow, Annie! That's sure is an expensive ride you got out there. You feel safe driving it around this neighborhood?"

"That's not my mom's car. That's Daniel's car!" Jordan proudly exclaimed before Annie could put a hand over her youngest son's mouth.

"What?! Daniel's got a car?" Cousin Terry screeched.

Suddenly, a line of Baileys traipsed outside to get a look at Daniel's blue Ford Escape. It wasn't quite the luxury car he hoped to get once he'd been on his job for several months, but it was shiny and new. And his alone, thanks to hard work, lots of overtime, and good credit.

As his father's family gathered around the vehicle, they asked their nosy questions—How much did it cost? What was the monthly payment? Did he have insurance? How much was the car insurance? Daniel's cousin, Manny, offered to get him a bogus car insurance card.

"But what if I get in a wreck? Who's gonna pay to get my car fixed?" Daniel asked to make Manny think, for once, of the consequences of illegal activity.

"You get in a wreck, just drive it to Uncle Jo's shop. He'll fix it for, like, half the cost. I mean, I'm just tryin' to save you some money every month, cuz. Insurance is a rip-off. Spend all that money, and you never even use it."

When they got back in the house, one of the younger cousins asked how much Jordan's shoes cost. Someone else would want to know if Annie's Coach bag was real. When it was determined that the purse wasn't a flea market knock-off, there was a collective agreement that Annie must be crazy to spend so much money on a purse—especially with Levi sitting in prison practically starving.

"You could put some money on his books, you know? And Daniel, now that you're making good money, it wouldn't hurt to send your father something every once in a while. You sure spend enough on clothes and a car, I see," Daniel's Aunt Kathleen forcefully suggested.

Annie took that as her cue to leave. "Well, it was nice seeing everyone again. You all have a Merry Christmas and a Happy New Year."

"Leaving so soon?" Grandma Bailey asked, taking a puff of her cigarette despite the hacking cough that overtook her after almost every drag. Her sandy blonde hair bounced violently with each series.

"Yeah, we'd better be heading on home now. Come here, Jordan, let me help you with your coat." Annie gave Grandma Bailey a hug and quickly left the trailer, which had suddenly become too stuffy.

Daniel hung behind a bit, walking through the room hugging these people he hardly knew. With Annie safely out of hearing distance, Grandma Bailey and Aunt Kathleen sprung the news on Daniel. "Your father is getting out of prison come the first of the year."

The whole room fell silent, as though they had all been anticipating this moment. Daniel was not sure how to respond. He didn't know Levi any more than he knew the people staring back at him. "Okay."

"Aren't you happy Uncle Levi is coming home?" Daniel's younger cousin, April, asked. She was probably seven years old; not much older than Jordan. Daniel figured April had probably never even laid eyes on Levi. After all, Daniel had only seen him twice—through smudged glass—in twenty years.

The thought of being around his father sent an eerie vibe through Daniel's tall, thin frame. Nonetheless, Daniel composed himself and answered April's question. "Yeah. That's...that's great."

Aunt Kathleen continued, "Your father is going to need some help when he gets out. Money, lots of love...even a place to stay. This neighborhood's too bad for him to hang around here without getting in trouble again."

Daniel's eyebrows lifted, the muscles around his mouth relaxed into a *What does this have to do with me?* expression.

"We were wondering if...since you have your own place now...Levi could stay with you when he gets out?" his aunt pressed. She folded her hands underneath her chin, almost as though praying.

Daniel looked at his grandmother now. He had those same gray eyes with brown flecks, but honestly those were the

11

only things they had in common besides Levi. He didn't know Grandma Bailey the same way he knew his mom's side of the family. All his life, his mother had been silent about his father. She let his character and his family speak for themselves. From what Daniel could tell, he was glad his mom didn't let his father's family influence him too much.

"Aunt Kathleen, I don't know about that—"

"He's got no place else to go, Daniel. Maybe if he spends some time with you, he might get back on track. And his parole officer would probably treat him better knowing he's with someone…well… a family member who doesn't have a record."

Daniel's first instincts took over. He shook his head. "No, I don't think that's a good idea. I mean, I don't even know my…Levi."

"He *is* your father," Grandma Bailey jumped in. "He gave you life. And the Bible says honor your father and your mother." She pointed at the faded picture of Jesus on the wall.

From the moans in the room, Daniel could tell that everyone agreed with Grandma Bailey and, apparently, God. Daniel couldn't understand what made them want to bring up the Bible now that they needed him, but not when it was time to refrain from stealing or setting up illegal insurance card schemes.

Grandma Bailey took another deadly puff of her cigarette, coughed a spell, then ordered, "April, hand me the Bible so I can show Daniel."

"That's okay, Grandma. I don't need to see it in the Bible, alright? I…I can't just move my father into my apartment. I don't even know him. I mean, what if he…isn't the same?" Not that Daniel had any point of reference in the first place.

12

Grandma spat through a round of coughs that sounded more like a machine gun going off. Then, she huffed, "At the rate I'm going, I don't have much time left, Daniel. I want to see my son settled before I die."

Seriously? She's playing the sick Grandma card?

"Daniel, your father loves you. Always has," Aunt Kathleen said softly as she touched Daniel's arm, diverting his attention from Grandma Bailey's antics. "Levi never got to show how much he cared for you before he went to prison. But now, he wants the opportunity to bond with you and be the father you never had. I know Annie was a great mom. But your dad...well...he was only seventeen when he got sent to prison for being in the wrong place at the wrong time with the wrong people. He made a mistake, Daniel. Just give him a chance."

Daniel kept silent all the way back to his mother's house, but inside his head, he screamed at himself. *Are you crazy?* The idea of letting his father move into his apartment was completely absurd, but Aunt Kathleen's point about the fact that his father was only a kid when he got sentenced had struck a nerve in Daniel.

Her pleas made Daniel remember the night he and a few of his friends had gone to a college party, drank themselves silly, and then Daniel had driven home under the influence of alcohol. He'd come within inches of running over a pedestrian downtown. Even though the man shouldn't have stepped out in front of the car, Daniel knew that if he'd hit the man, he would have been charged, jailed, and possibly imprisoned simply because he'd been drinking. And if the man had died as a result of the accident, Daniel could have been behind bars for twenty years just like his dad. Good thing the man had the quick senses to hop back on the curb just in the nick of time.

Since that night, Daniel hadn't touched alcohol. He made the decision to turn his life around. Daniel spent eight months at the Cleveland Job Corps, learning his field, and got a job that paid the bills and kept him out of trouble—not to mention helping people. He thanked his lucky stars for a second chance to make the right decision. Levi, however, hadn't been so lucky. When he really thought things through, Daniel realized that he could have easily been in his father's shoes. He had no room to judge.

Annie didn't press Daniel in the car, on account of Jordan's presence. But as soon as they reached home, she sent the boy upstairs to change into pajamas and go to bed. Annie sat next to Daniel on the couch and fired her own questions.

"What did they say?"

He hesitated for a moment. *Should I tell her or not?* If he didn't, she'd badger him until he made up some kind of lie to get her off his back. But if he told her the truth, maybe she could offer him some advice. Maybe she knew something about the man her father used to be that might help him make a solid decision.

"They said my dad gets out of prison next month. They wanted to know if I would let him live with me."

Annie's forehead wrinkled and she sucked in her chin. "Live with *you*? Are they *crazy*?"

"Yeah," Daniel said with an uneasy chuckle in his voice.

"Wait a minute," his mother said, squinting her eyes. "You're not actually considering this arrangement, are you?"

"No. I mean, I don't know. Aunt Kathleen said he's sure to go back to jail if he moves back to the old neighborhood."

"That's not your problem, Daniel. Your dad is an adult. He can choose to do the right thing or not."

"But if he had a place to stay, away from his old surroundings, that would make things easier."

"Easier!" his mother shrieked. "You think it's *easy* raising two boys on my own? You think it was *easy* to change my life the moment I got pregnant with you? You think it's *easy* to work two jobs instead of getting caught up in a cycle of poverty on government assistance? Everybody wants it *easy* these days."

Somehow, every time his mother got angry, she threw up the fact that she'd maintained their household without food stamps or child support. She gave all the credit to the fact that she'd quickly dropped out of school, gotten her GED, and then a cosmetology license after she found out she was pregnant with Daniel her senior year in high school.

"But Mom, you *did* have help. Grams kept me during the day so you could go to work and save money. If she hadn't been there for you, you would have had to pay rent and daycare, and you would've needed help from the government to do all that."

Annie looked her son in the eyes. "Yes, Grams helped me because I made a mistake. But I wasn't a *criminal*. There's a difference."

"Is that all my father was to you? A criminal?"

"Of course not, Daniel. Your dad was funny and smart. Too smart for his own good, which is why he never thought he'd get caught selling drugs. But he did. And when he and his friends got busted, instead of throwing their hands up in the air, one of them shot the cop."

"But my father wasn't the one who pulled the trigger." Daniel surprised himself with the defense.

"He still got the same charge, though. As far as the law is

concerned, he's a murderer," Annie argued.

"He couldn't have been that bad, Mom. You were in a relationship with him right before he got arrested."

Annie shook her head. "Yeah, but I didn't know he was selling drugs. Anyway, none of that matters now. Listen, Daniel, even if your father wasn't a hardened criminal before he went to prison, he is one by now.

"You remember your Cousin Charles? Remember how crazy he was when he got out of prison? He shot his girlfriend, stole his own mother's money. People don't know how to act when they get out of prison. I'm sorry. I'm not trying to talk bad about your father—you know I never have—but he's an ex-con, now. He can't be trusted. I don't want you to risk messing up your life by getting involved with him."

"Mom, I'm twenty years old. I know how to keep myself out of trouble. And besides, I...never even got to know my father."

"You don't have to move him into your apartment in order to establish a relationship with him. You can call him on the phone, text him, visit him at Grandma Bailey's, meet him at McDonald's or something. Just don't let him move in with you, for goodness sake."

Daniel stood up from the couch and pulled his jeans to his waist.

"I wish you wouldn't sag your pants, Daniel. Makes you look like a thug," his mother fussed. She always nagged him about the pants thing, but now that he was out of the house, she couldn't do anything about it. At the pharmacy, he wore his khaki pants in a professional manner. Away from the job, he dressed however he wanted. He prided himself on knowing how to operate in two different worlds. Maybe if his dad learned how to be bi-cultural, too, he could blend back into society.

Daniel ran upstairs to tuck Jordan in bed and then back down again to kiss his mother good-bye.

"Son, don't do anything foolish."

"I won't, Mom. Trust me. I got this."

As soon as Daniel walked through Grandma Bailey's doorway, one thing was for certain: Daniel looked just like his father, minus dozens of tattoos and twenty years of hard time. An array of facial scars and a slight limp told the story of Levi's dog-eat-dog life behind bars.

"Hey, son," Levi called as he hobbled into the living room with arms outstretched.

Daniel avoided looking at his father directly. "Just call me Daniel."

Levi dropped his arms to his side and, instead, took note of Daniel's gesture for a simple, impersonal handshake.

"You got your stuff?"

"Yeah. It's not much." Levi smacked the light backpack. "Toothbrush, pair of shoes, couple of shirts, pants, and underclothes your Aunt Kathleen bought me."

"Okay. Let's go."

"Thank you so much, Daniel," Grandma Bailey yelled between gasps for air. Quickly, she replaced the oxygen mask over her nose and mouth. "You granted one of your Grandma's last wishes."

Daniel could only hope that spending time with Levi would bring about one of his *first* wishes—to have a father in his life.

Levi lay low the first few weeks at Daniel's house. He was enamored by the Internet, and fascinated by the abundance of reality TV shows. He took extra long, super-hot showers just because he could.

Daniel made it his business to spend as much time away from the apartment as possible. Levi made him uncomfortable. Every sentence Levi spoke contained at least two forms of profanity, and he got so angry at the people on television that he'd stormed out of the room on several occasions.

Levi didn't seem interested in catching up on lost time. Basically, he only talked directly to Daniel when he needed help filling out an application on the Internet. McDonalds, Wendy's, Home Depot. All the while, Levi cussed and ranted about how stupid it was for people to fill out applications online. "This whole world's gone mad," was followed by another set of expletives. Then, "Done nothing all day but look at this stupid screen. How am I supposed to get a job when they can't even look me in the eye?"

The few times both men had occasion to sit down at the kitchen table, Levi mumbled and complained about how hard things were on the outside and how no one wanted to hire him.

"No offense, Levi, but we are in the middle of an economic recession. Even people who haven't been to prison are having a hard time finding jobs," Daniel offered.

Levi grumbled, "You don't know what you're talking about. You ain't ever had it hard. Your momma made your life so easy. All you do is put on your little tan pants and your red shirt, or sometimes a suit, go to work, and come home every day without breaking a sweat. Pharmacy tech? What kind of job is that for a man?

"And I haven't even seen you with a woman. What's up with you?"

Daniel looked down into his plate of chicken Alfredo and took a deep breath. His father was trying to push his buttons, but Daniel wouldn't fall for it. He'd read online that this was how men dealt with each other in prison. They bullied one another to maintain manhood. The article said that if Daniel remained calm and didn't respond to the newly freed man's attacks, his father would soon learn that he didn't have to constantly assert himself.

"All I'm saying is that you need to be patient," Daniel reiterated calmly.

They sat in silence for another minute before Levi set his fork on the table. "Look at me."

For the first time, Daniel took his father head-on. "Yeah?"

His father folded his leathery hands and put them under his chin. "You think the world is fair?"

Daniel shrugged. "No. Probably not."

"You think I got a fair shake in life?"

"No." Daniel kept a straight face.

"You ever thought about..." His father shook his head. "Forget it. I gotta get out of here."

"Why?"

"'Cause you're a good kid, Daniel. You're too good for me."

Confused, Daniel asked, "Levi, what are you talking about?"

"You...you got it all figured out. Got your nice place, your nice car. You play by the rules, do everything by the book. Just like your momma. She's made you a yes-man, a white-collar company boy. You've never worked hard a day in your life."

"Dude, you don't know me or my mother," Daniel snapped back. He didn't care if his father insulted *him*, but his mother was off limits. "I've been working since I was fourteen. I've gotten up at five in the morning to ride my bike all over the neighborhood throwing newspapers. I've gone door-to-door asking people if I could mow their lawns in the summer heat. After working hard for all those different people, I figured out I could make far more money by using my head, so I went to job corps when I finished high school. Busted my butt in my trade classes, worked hard in my TABE classes, put up with all those rules, kept my focus. And my mom worked hard to make sure I didn't fall into the same trap you did. So don't talk to me about not working hard."

Levi put both hands on his knees and pushed himself to a standing position. "You got your way of doing things, Daniel, and I've got mine. Take me back to your grandmother's house."

Daniel threw his napkin on the table. "Why? I mean, I'm doing everything I can to help you get back on your feet."

Levi raised his hand as he left the kitchen area. "I don't want your help. I have to find my own way."

Daniel followed his father to the small living area and watched Levi stuff his few belongings into the backpack.

He watched his father hobble to the bathroom, grab his toothbrush and slip it into the front pocket of his bag.

Daniel grabbed his keys from the coffee table and, in frustration, walked to his car. He escorted his father back to Grandma Bailey's neighborhood. The more they drove, the less Daniel cared. If his father didn't want a relationship with him, whatever. He wasn't going to cry about it. He'd made it this long without Levi, he'd make it through the next 20 years, no problem. All he could do from this point on was be a good role model for Jordan. Maybe, one of these days, he'd have a son of his own. He'd be a great dad.

As they rounded the corner to Grandma Bailey's place, Daniel noticed Levi's restlessness. He'd put his hand on the door handle and unlatched his seatbelt as though he wanted to hop out before they reached the driveway. Daniel had barely put the car in park when Levi got out and slammed the door behind him.

"Hey, wait a minute," Daniel said, killing the engine and getting out of the car. "What's wrong with you?" If this was his last time seeing his father, Daniel wanted some answers.

"Nothing. Good-bye. Have a nice life. Trust me. I'm doing you a favor. You're better off without me," he yelled over his shoulder at Daniel.

"What's your problem, Levi?"

Daniel trailed him into Grandma Bailey's house, where a room full of relatives met them both with blank stares.

"What's wrong?" Aunt Kathleen asked.

Grandma Bailey rolled her eyes and focused on the television again.

"I can't stay with him." Levi waved toward Daniel and disappeared in a back room.

"What happened?" Aunt Kathleen directed her question at Daniel.

"He just said he couldn't stay with me anymore."

"Why?"

"Said I was too good."

Manny sprang off the couch and wrapped an arm around Daniel's shoulder. "Come here, cuz." He pulled Daniel outside and whispered into his ear, "I guess Uncle Levi didn't get around to asking you a huge favor."

Daniel wondered what favor could be bigger than asking to live with someone. "What?"

"See, we got this guy. On the streets. Big Ray. Said he could get us some real money for, you know, some of the stuff at your job. Just to hold Uncle Levi over until he can find work."

Daniel eased out of Manny's grasp. "What?"

"Yeah. Some of those depression pills, stuff like that. Sells real quick with people who can actually afford to pay, you know what I'm sayin'? And you got the best way to get it, working at the pharmacy. You can take a little at a time without anybody knowing."

Daniel couldn't believe his ears. "My father wanted me to steal from my job?"

Manny raised his eyebrows and sighed. "He didn't want you to steal, he just wanted you to help him get ahead, you know? But I guess he didn't ask…so somebody has to."

"I'm leaving," Daniel said as he walked back to his car.

Manny followed, practically begging, "Aw come on, man! You've never helped this family! You and your T-Jones always act like you're too good for us!"

Daniel turned up the music so loud he couldn't hear Manny's cussing as he backed out of Grandma Bailey's driveway.

His mother was right after all. Now, Daniel's only wish was to forget about his father forever.

After Reading – "First and Last Wish"
1. Would you have advised Daniel to let his father move in with him?
2. What lesson do you think Daniel will learn from this situation?
3. What do Levi's actions say about how he feels about Daniel?
4. Do you think Daniel should continue to keep in touch with the Bailey family?

Writing Prompts
1. Create a presentation showing programs that help a certain population (ex-cons, recovering addicts, high school drop-outs, etc.) get back on the right track.
2. Write an essay about the different between "helping" and "enabling" people.

He Loves Me, He Loves Me, Too

Words (in order of appearance)	Definition	Example Sentence
Publicity	Attention from people	She faked pregnancy in order to gain publicity before her CD release.
Rhetorical	A question asked without expecting an answer	When my mother gives me a lecture, she asks lots of rhetorical questions.
Signature (adj.)	Unique	My sister wears her signature scarf with everything.
Nuisance	A person, situation, or thing that bothers you	The clock's ticking is a nuisance that keeps me from getting sleep.
Retrospect	Looking back over the past with greater insight	In retrospect, I wish I had studied more so my GPA would be higher.
Rescind	Take back or change a decision	When she got into the fight, they rescinded her award.
Unfounded	Not based on facts	The judge found him innocent because the claims were unfounded.
Notion	Idea	I don't know how she got the notion that we were going out.
Traumatized	Shocked by an incident that affects you for a long time	She was so traumatized by the car accident that she refused to drive again for months.
expunge	Removed information from an official record	If he stays out of trouble, they will expunge his file.

Before Reading – "He Loves Me, He Loves Me, Too"
1. What makes a player a player? Are players heartless?
2. Have you ever had to choose between two potential romantic interests? If so, what criteria did you use to choose the right one?
3. Should teens get involved in serious relationships?
4. Why do people pick on people whom they perceive as "different"?

Yellow Girl
Your smile, your hair
Everything about you
Is Yellow.
Yellow is life,
Yellow is the sun,
Yellow is how I feel
When I see you.
Smile, Sunshine!

Bria Hopkins folded the poem and placed it in her purse. It was the third one this week from "the new boy" Kaleb Langston. The usual newcomer excitement was still buzzing around their mid-sized school, and Bria was riding high on the increased popularity of being the one Kaleb liked. This publicity could come in very handy when it was time for student council elections. The more people heard her name, the better.

"Where's he from? Does he play any sports?" the cheerleaders wanted to know. "Is he smart? What's his G-P-A?" the competitive A-P crowd wanted to know. Bria couldn't answer those questions just yet. In truth, the only thing she knew about Kaleb was that he liked to write poems. Aside from giving him a smile and a thank-you, she really hadn't talked to him because he always rushed out of every class they had together without saying a word.

Another positive side effect was the fact that Bria's ex-boyfriend, Devon, was suddenly re-interested in her. "I hear you got a new man now," he assumed as he followed her to the student parking lot Thursday after school.

Bria just smiled to herself and pressed the remote to unlock her door.

Devon huffed, "Oh, it's like that now?"

"Why do you care anyway?" Bria asked. "*You* broke up with *me*, remember?"

"See, you didn't even have to go there." Devon stepped away from the car so that Bria could shut the driver's door.

She started the car and put the gear in drive. Though she didn't look at Devon directly, she could see him standing there, waiting for her to roll down the window. Devon was wrong for breaking up, and he didn't deserve to know what was going on in her life, but the truth was: Bria was still very much in love with him.

Maybe Kaleb's attention was the spotlight Devon needed to recognize what a great girlfriend Bria had been. They say you don't really know what you've lost until someone else finds it. Well, Devon was learning that lesson the hard way, and Bria was enjoying every minute of it.

Devon knocked on the window and, slowly, Bria lowered it - an inch. Bria looked straight ahead because if she gazed into Devon's hazel eyes, she would melt. "What do you want, Devon?"

"I want to talk," he claimed.

Bria turned on the radio and, as if on cue, the chorus line FROM Rihanna's *Take a Bow* played: *That was quite a show – very entertaining.* The song reminded Bria of how heartbroken she had been when Devon ended their relationship.

Her emotions got the best of her. She faced Devon and blurted out, "You know what hurt the most? You never even really gave me a real reason why you broke up. I know we only went out for a few months, but you could have at least told me why."

Devon looked away now, above the hood of her car. This was Bria's worst fear. He didn't have a real reason. She just wasn't good enough anymore. Or maybe those rumors about him and Jazmyn Jones were true – maybe he really had been cheating on her all along.

Before she could work up enough anger to drive away, Devon looked back down at Bria again. The moment Bria had been avoiding – the moment their eyes met – was every bit as draining as she knew it would be. "Can you just...roll the window down a little more?"

Bria surrendered and Devon leaned into her car. "Can we talk about this later? I have to go to football practice."

Now it was Bria's turn to look away. "Whatever."

"Hey," Devon said as he gently pulled her chin back toward himself. Then he pecked her slightly on the lips. "I'll call you later."

She watched Devon jog back toward the football field and wondered how on earth a boy could be so hot. She and Devon were opposites in many ways – he was the jock, she was the student council type – but they'd made a good couple, or so she thought.

Well, she couldn't worry about it now. She had tons of homework ahead of her, not to mention church. Bria focused her attention to the road and let her foot off the brake. She looked to her left and her right, then stepped on the brake again at the sight of Kaleb, about fifty feet away. He was sitting on top of his car, writing.

Bria wondered how long he had been sitting there and if

he had seen what happened between her and Devon. She waited for a momenT, hoping he would look up, but he didn't. She tapped her horn to get his attention. He gave a quick glance and returned to his writing.

"That was weird," Bria said to herself.

The next day, Bria came to school with much attitude. Church lasted longer than usual, which meant she'd stayed up until almost 2 a.m. finishing an assignment that Mr. Daniels decided he wasn't even going to collect. What she was most angry about, however, was the fact that Devon didn't call like he said he would.

When her best friend, Amber, asked Bria about her funky mood during lunch, Bria declared, "Devon is now officially out of my life."

"When did he get back *in?*"

"He tried to get back in the picture yesterday, but it's over," Bria replied with a sigh as she slung a cheeseburger onto her tray.

"Okay, don't take it out on the food," Amber laughed. "I told you Devon was a player – I don't even know why you let him waste your precious time."

Bria admitted, "'Cause he's hot."

"You've got a point," Amber quickly agreed.

Both girls paid for their food and drifted over to their usual corner of the cafeteria, speaking to mutual friends and catching up on school gossip. Halfway into their meal, Amber whispered to Bria, "Don't look now. Here comes Mr. Unreliable."

Devon walked right by their table without even looking at Bria. And the reason why wasn't far behind. Jazmyn called out to him, "Hold up, Devon!" He slowed his pace long enough to allow Jazmyn to catch up with him, then he passed on by.

"Am I not sitting right here?" Bria asked rhetorically.

"Yes, you are," Amber answered.

"I am too through with him." Bria watched as Jazmyn walked across the cafeteria with Devon. They weren't holding hands, but Jazmyn was rubbing all up against him like a dog marking its territory. It was a setback for women everywhere, as far as Bria was concerned; an outright insult to both Palin and Hillary.

Sixth period history was boring, as usual, but everyone watched the war film out of respect for classmates who had family members serving in the military. The only one who didn't seem to be watching the film was Kaleb. He was busy watching Bria. She never could quite catch him looking at her, but she had that feeling, the inexplicable tingle that comes from being watched.

When class was over, Kaleb rushed by her, dropping a piece of paper on her desk.

For You
He doesn't deserve
Such beauty,
Such wit.
He's not good enough
For You.

Can anyone deserve you?
Probably not.
No one is good enough
For You.

But I
Would take a class
And pass a test
To prove myself
Good enough
For You.

Because there's nothing
Nothing
I wouldn't do
For You.

When Bria showed Amber the poem after school, Amber's response was, "Bria, I hope you don't take this the wrong way. You've got the whole naturally cute thing going on, but you ain't no Helen of Troy. It's something wrong with this boy. I mean, this poem thing has gotten out of hand."

"What?" Bria shrieked. "Just because a guy writes a girl a poem doesn't mean there's something wrong with him! Rap songs are nothing but poems, but nobody seems to think Jay-Z is crazy."

"If Jay-Z made a song out of *this* poem, he *would* be crazy for real," Amber laughed as they exited the school building.

Just then, Devon crept up and hugged Bria from behind. She smelled his intoxicating cologne before she saw his face, and it took everything in her to act annoyed. "What are you doing?" Bria shrugged him off.

"Shouldn't you be somewhere getting ready for a football game?" Amber asked.

Devon replied, "It's a bye week - no game tonight."

"Where's your *girl*?" Bria snapped.

Devon returned the question, "Where's your *man*?"

"I ain't got no man."

"I ain't got no girl."

Bria rolled her eyes. "Whatever."

Devon noticed the paper in Bria's hands. "What's that?" he asked.

Quickly, she folded the note and put it in her back pocket. "None of your business."

Amber spilled the beans. "It's a beautiful love poem from Kaleb. Something you wouldn't, or *couldn't*, write."

Devon dismissed Amber with a wave. "I can't write no stupid poem 'cause I ain't gay." He laughed at his own joke.

Bria countered, "Please, Devon. You do not have to be gay to write a poem."

Devon stopped and tapped a finger on his chin, as though he was thinking. Then he simply replied, "Uh, yeah. You do."

The three students continued walking the path in front of the building side by side, heading toward the parking lot. Bria saw Kaleb walking toward them and silently thanked fate for setting up this encounter. Kaleb eyed her, ignoring Devon and Amber completely. His light brown skin was flawless and his deep brown eyes were piercing – something Bria hadn't noticed because he never looked at her long enough for her to actually appreciate them.

As she passed Kaleb, Bria flirted, "Thanks for the poem, Kaleb."

"I meant every word." He kept walking toward his car.

Amber cracked up. "Dang! He said he meant that, girl!" She slapped hands with Bria. "I gotta go. I'll catch up with you tomorrow."

Devon was outraged. He turned back and confronted Kaleb. "Man, how you just gon' disrespect me like that?"

Kaleb kept walking, ignoring Devon completely.

"I know you heard me!" Devon yelled. When Kaleb didn't respond, Devon topped it off with, "See, I told you he ain't nothin' but a punk."

Kaleb hopped into his car and sped off.

"Why did you have to do that to him?" Bria confronted Devon. "He's just a nice guy."

"What, you like him or something?"

Bria shrugged her shoulders, finally reaching her car.

"Answer me!" Devon demanded.

Bria blew up in his face. "Why don't you answer a few questions for me, like why you walked by me today in the cafeteria with Jazmyn Jones! You acted like you didn't even know I existed. Is *she* the reason you broke up with me, Devon? Huh? And why didn't you call me last night? I thought we were supposed to be talking through our problems!"

"I can't talk to you when you got some other dude writin' you poems."

"One thing at a time," Bria cornered him. "You and Jazmyn today in the cafeteria. What was that?"

"Nothing!"

Bria stopped and studied his face. He was lying. She could tell by the way his lips were shaking. Though she could almost feel her heart breaking, Bria pronounced, "Devon, you're full of it."

"Oh, so you gon' just kick me to the curb for some gay dude?" Devon taunted her.

Bria hopped into her car, started the engine, and repeated the previous day's routine by rolling down the window just an

35

inch. "No. I'm kicking you to the curb because of *you*. See ya."

Bria turned up the radio and took off without giving Devon a chance to make a comeback– not that he had one good enough to change her mind. She looked in the rear-view mirror and saw him pointing at her, yelling like somebody crazy.

The homecoming game was just around the corner. Already, two guys had asked Bria to go with them. One of the invitations came from a guy named Chaz in her science class. Bria hadn't answered him yet – she was holding out to see if someone she actually liked was going to ask. The other invitation came from Kaleb in his signature style:

One Night
One night of fall-crisp winds,
A football game
And folly.

One night of celebration and tradition
Of courts and queens
And kings.

One night of remembering
Those past acquaintances
And friends.

One night – homecoming night
The night of reunions Is all I ask.

Would do me the pleasure,
The honor,
Of this One Night?

But by this point, the poems were nothing more than a nuisance to Bria. Now that everyone had written Kaleb off as a weirdo (partly thanks to Devon), Bria wasn't interested in him. In retrospect, Bria wasn't sure that she was ever truly interested in Kaleb. She'd only accepted his poems because she didn't want to be rude. Well, that plus they made Devon jealous. Still, she didn't want to turn down Kaleb's invitation just yet. If push came to shove and Chaz got another date in the next few days, Bria would be stuck out. She would rather go with Kaleb than with no one. After all, every girl wants a mum.

Several days had passed since that crazy day in the parking lot. Bria and Devon hadn't said two words to each other. They only gave each other evil glares in the hallways – when Jazmyn wasn't looking.

"Why don't you two just sit down and talk," Amber suggested one day after watching the silent exchange between Bria and Devon in the hallway.

"Psh, I ain't got nothing to say to him," Bria snapped. "It's over."

"No, it isn't," Amber singsonged. "You still like him and you know it. Otherwise, you would have already accepted the invitation from Chaz or Kaleb."

As the two friends continued walking down the hallway to their last period class together, Bria agreed, "I don't like either one of them. I'll give it another couple of days - see if somebody better comes along."

Two days went by and nothing happened by way of

homecoming invitations, so Bria was forced to make a choice. She found Chaz before school started, but he had to rescind his invitation. "I'm sorry, Bria. I had to hurry up and put in the order for the mum. I'm going with Sorna."

"It's cool," Bria said. "I understand." She had to admit to herself that she was a little wrong for leaving Chaz hanging.

Bria knew that she couldn't top Kaleb's poems, but she tried:

Reply to: One Night

> *One night of friendship,*
> *One night of fun,*
> *One night of smiles,*
> *Am I the one?*
> *Yes.*
> *So throw your hands in the air!*
> *And wave 'em like you just don't care!*

She gave him the lame poem in sixth period, and Kaleb cracked up laughing in the middle of the teacher's lecture. All of a sudden, it was like Kaleb opened up to her. When the bell rang, he initiated the phone-number swap. Kaleb called her later that night, and Bria was pleasantly surprised to know that he held a very intriguing conversation. Kaleb was good people, even if he was a little weird.

"So, why are you always writing poems?"

"My mother is a writer. I guess I got it from her," he said. "I grew up with books and writing and words just like some kids grow up with music and TV. What did you grow up with?"

That was an easy question for Bria. "Church."

Kaleb laughed. "Seriously? You go to church?"

"Yeah," Bria said, a little offended. "Who *doesn't* go to church?"

"I guess me," Kaleb joked.

"Well, you should go some time."

"I'll think about it."

Bria's phone beeped and she looked at the caller ID. Devon? Why would he be calling her? "Kaleb, I've gotta go."

"Alright. I'll see you tomorrow – we can talk about where you'd like to go eat after the game."

"Okay. Bye."

Bria switched calls. "What do you want?"

"Bria," Devon's voice came through in a peculiar tone that alarmed his ex-girlfriend.

"What's wrong?"

"My foot," he nearly cried, "I hurt it real bad in practice today. The doctor says I can't play next week. I probably can't play again until homecoming, at the earliest."

Bria suddenly forgot how much she couldn't stand Devon. Instead, she remembered how much he loved football. "I'm so sorry, Devon."

"You're the only person I know who goes to church and stuff. So, I need you to pray for me," he confessed.

"Okay – definitely," Bria quickly agreed.

Devon continued, "And I'm sorry about everything, okay? You were right about Jazmyn. I was…she was trying to get in my head, but I see now that she's not the girl I need. You are, Bria. I love *you*."

Bria's heart almost stopped. For the past three months, she had been waiting to hear those three words from Devon. "I

39

love you, too, Devon. Where are you?"

"I'm at home right now. You want to come over?"

"I can't. It's too late. You want me to pick you up for school tomorrow?" she offered.

"No. The doctor put me on pain medication and told me I can't put any weight on my foot for the next couple of days," he informed her.

"Okay. I'll take good notes for you in English class," Bria said.

"Dang," Devon gasped, "that's why I love you – you take care of business, girl. Say – you still with old gay boy?"

"He is *not* gay," Bria defended her new friend from this unfounded notion.

"Whatever. I don't want you hanging with him anymore. No more poems, no more of him looking at you, nothing," Devon insisted. "It's just me and you now, okay?"

Bria hesitated.

Devon repeated, "Okay?"

"Okay."

Bria planned to find Kaleb first thing the next day and tell him that she couldn't go to homecoming with him. Easier said than done.

When she saw Kaleb's smiling face and he complimented her hair and clothes, Bria's resolve was put on hold. Devon never told Bria she looked good – at least not in any kind of respectful way. He had made some suggestive remarks about her body, but that was it.

Still, she had promised Devon that she would end it with Kaleb. She had to keep her word. Just when she had mustered up enough courage to tell Kaleb the truth, he threw her off track. "So, when do people go to church? Sundays, right?"

"Yeah, Sunday. Listen, Kaleb—"

"I think I'll give it a shot," he interrupted her. "I told my mom about it, and she said she never really made me go to church because she wanted me to make up my own mind about God and religion and stuff."

"That's good. I need to tell, you, though—"

"So, you think God is…like…God?"

His question stopped Bria cold. She replied passionately, "Of course He is."

Kaleb nodded. "All right, okay. I never met anybody who was so convinced of it. Someone who actually stood up for God and all these things that are supposed to be right, you know? You were the only person who even smiled at me the first day I got here. And you were the only one who didn't treat me like an outsider. So I'm thinking – maybe this God stuff is true after all."

Bria sighed. "It is true."

Kaleb smiled. "I'll see you later." And he took off jogging, obviously trying to beat the bell.

When lunchtime came, Bria didn't feel much like eating. Her brain seemed to weight a million pounds.

"You gonna eat your fries?" Amber asked, eyeing the untouched food on Bria's Styrofoam plate.

"No. Go ahead."

Through a mouth full of food, Amber admonished Bria. "You've gotta tell Kaleb the truth. It's the right thing to do."

"You know, maybe it's not the right thing to do. I mean, Kaleb and I can go to the game as friends," Bria tried to reason.

"Devon is not going to let you go to the homecoming

game with Kaleb. And trust me, Kaleb is not interested in just being your friend."

Bria thought for a moment, replaying the previous night's conversation with Devon in her head. If he hadn't hurt his foot, he wouldn't have thought twice about her. And if she hadn't been feeling so sorry for him, she wouldn't have agreed to be his girl again. Their whole relationship was based on fear, guilt, and pity. And Devon's extreme hotness. But this thing with Kaleb...well...it could be better. Based on respect. Intelligence. They might even start going to church together.

"Amber," Bria announced, "I'm not going to cancel my homecoming date with Kaleb."

Amber's eyes got real wide and her bottom lip dropped. "And what are you going to do about Devon?"

Bria sighed. "I don't know. I've got a few days before Devon comes back to school. Maybe by then I'll have a better idea of which boy I like most. I need to be able to make an informed choice."

"Hmmm," Amber smacked. "You ever heard the word *player?*"

"I am *not* playing them!" Bria defended herself. "I just can't make up my mind right now, that's all."

"Spoken like a true player."

Bria rolled her eyes at Amber. "Whatever. Besides, you know what they say. Don't hate the player. Hate the game."

Amber shook her head, laughing at Bria's joke. "You know you ain't no player 'cause you sure ain't got no game." And they both laughed because it was true.

It didn't take Bria two days to figure out that Kaleb was the winner. He was nice, he was a gentleman, and he was even able to help her with homework – something that never happened with Devon. When she talked to Kaleb on the phone, he asked her serious questions like who she would vote for if she could and which college she wanted to attend. There was always a hint of flirting in their conversations, but it was clear to Bria that Kaleb liked her for who she was. He liked her personality, her brain, and he even had an appreciation for her faith.

All she had to do now was break the news to Devon.

Bria hadn't talked to Devon much because every time she called, his mom said that Devon was asleep due to the pain medication. "He'll be back in school Thursday," Devon's mom had said. So when Thursday rolled around, Bria was ready. No second thoughts.

Finding Devon, however, proved an impossible feat. She finally asked one of his teammates, Maurice, where Devon was. Maurice told her that Devon hadn't come to school. Bria's shoulders dropped as she looked toward the sky. How much longer would she have to wait to break up with Devon so she wouldn't have to feel like she was cheating on Kaleb?

Thursday after school, Kaleb met Bria at her car. They stood around flirting as she tried to convince him to come with her to Bible study at church. "It'll be fun," she smiled as he pulled her closely. Bria let herself fall into Kaleb's embrace.

"I suppose it couldn't hurt anything."

She looked up at him. "You serious?"

"Yeah."

"I'm so excited for you," she said with a smile. Then Bria hoisted herself up on her tip-toes and planted a kiss on Kaleb's full lips.

He smiled. "I think I'll go to church Sunday, too."

She played his game, giving him another kiss.

Kaleb continued, "I'm thinking about becoming a pastor."

Bria playfully hit him and laughed at his witty joke. They were so engrossed with each other that neither of them saw Maurice and Devon pull up beside Bria's car. It was silly the way Devon almost broke his neck trying to get out of the Maurice's car so quickly with those heavy wooden crutches.

"Bria, I thought I told you not to mess with him," Devon yelled, breathless from his struggle.

Bria shook her head. "Devon, don't act crazy, okay?"

"Naw – you got some explaining to do. Why you out here all up on this gay dude?"

Kaleb defended himself. "You got one more time to call me gay."

Devon straightened up as much as possible. "What? You gon' wait 'til I'm in crutches to speak up for yourself?"

Maurice, who was still sitting in his car, yelled to Devon, "Man, D, come on. Let's go see coach."

"Naw, this gay fool wanna talk noise, I wanna see what he can do."

Bria jumped in. "Well, he's *obviously* doing something right. I'm with him – not you. Goodbye, Devon. It's over between me and you."

Devon gave Bria a look of disgust. "So you gon' pick *him* over *me*?"

Bria's silence spoke louder than words.

"Alright." Devon spoke as though he had a nasty taste in his mouth. "You wanna be with a punk, be with a punk."

Kaleb responded. "Well, if a punk can take your woman, what does that make you?"

Maurice clapped and laughed from inside his car. "Oh!

He got you on that one, D! Ha!"

Kaleb gave Devon a smirk, shook his head, and turned his back to walk away.

That's when it happened. Devon balanced himself on one foot, lifted one of the crutches in the air, and brought it crashing down on the back of Kaleb's head. Instantly, Kaleb crumbled to the ground.

"Oh my God!" Bria screamed as she lowered herself to Kaleb's side. "Oh my God!" Blood spilled from Kaleb's head, and his limbs began to twitch. She looked up at Devon. "Are you crazy?" In that moment, she saw the fear in Devon's eyes.

Maurice got out of the car to assess the damage. "Dang! Man, you didn't have to hit him like that!"

"I-I-I didn't th-think I swung that hard," Devon stuttered.

Bria pulled out her cell phone and called 9-1-1. She took off her jacket, balled it up and applied pressure to Kaleb's wound. "Hello. We need an ambulance at Northway High School. A boy got hit in the back of the head by another boy."

"Is the victim conscious?" The operator asked.

"No."

"Is he breathing?"

Bria cried, "I don't know. Just hurry up."

"Is the perpetrator still on the scene?"

Bria focused on Devon now. She wanted him to see and hear her answer. "Yes. The perpetrator is here on the scene."

"We'll send an ambulance and police right away."

The word around the school was that Devon Wilkerson and "the new boy" got into a fight over Bria Hopkins. Once again, everyone was trying to get information from Bria. "Did you set them up against each other?" "Which one were you going out with?" Bria was so traumatized by what happened that she really couldn't answer the questions.

Amber finally stepped in and began to act as Bria's spokesperson. She tried to tell everyone that it wasn't Bria's fault, but there was truly no stopping the speculation. By the end of school Friday, many of the students and teachers believed that Bria Hopkins had lured a gay guy to the parking lot so that two football players could beat him up.

Bria tried to visit Kaleb, but his parents didn't want her there. "I think you've caused enough trouble already, young lady," Kaleb's father said as he closed the hospital room door in Bria's face.

Even Mrs. Wilkerson had called Bria's cell phone and left a nasty message because Devon was in serious legal trouble.

Some of Bria's church friends also went to Northway High School, so now there was a whole new rumor about Bria going out with two different guys and one of them owed the other guy some money.

It was ridiculous for a while. Eventually, though, the rumors died down. Kaleb recovered and went to another school, and Devon plea bargained to a lesser charge that would be expunged from his record when he turned twenty-one.

But Bria's life would never be the same. She had a hard time forgiving herself. She figured that somehow, some way, she could have done something to prevent this from happening.

So when another "new boy" enrolled at their school and sat down next to Bria in class, she didn't do anything but look straight ahead.

After Reading – "He Loves Me, He Loves Me, Too"
1. Was Bria a player?
2. Did you agree that Kaleb was the best choice for Bria?
3. Could she have done anything to prevent the violent climax?
4. In your opinion, was there a coward in this story?
5. Should Bria feel guilty about what happened between Kaleb and Devon?

Writing Prompts
1. Write a letter from one character to another, one year after the story ends. It can be from Kaleb to Bria, from Maurice to Kaleb, from Kaleb's parents to Bria – any combination.
2. Write a how-to guide for choosing a date.
3. Write an essay on the importance of being honest with the people you care about.

Unlucky

Words (in order of appearance)	Definition	Example Sentence
entourage	A group of people following or traveling with a very important person	President Obama's entourage accompanied him to England.
cubicle	A small area in a room enclosed by a wall or partition	The employees worked quietly in their cubicles.
hoopla	Public attention or excitement about something	There was so much hoopla surrounding the event, we knew we needed to get there early.
nuisance	Something or someone that annoys or causes a problem	Although some household pests aren't dangerous, they are still a nuisance.
morph	To change appearance	Seemingly overnight, the girl morphed into a young lady.

Before Reading – "Unlucky"

1. Do you believe that some people are born lucky and others are born unlucky?
2. What do you do when you see someone who looks as though they have suffered physical trauma?
3. Have you ever teased someone for how they look? Have you ever been teased about your appearance?

I'm used to people staring at me. I understand why little kids do it—they've never seen anything quite like this. But teenagers and grown-ups should know better. By the time you're fifteen or twenty, you've had a few encounters with burn victims, amputees and the like. I know I look different from everyone else. Sometimes, that's the way the cards fall. Every once in a while, somebody's got to be born unlucky. Be glad it was me and not you.

Britt Culverhouse walked into his third period class along with his usual entourage of the school's most valuable male athletes. Of course, girls followed. Pretty girls. The kinds of girls who could have been in music videos if they had the right connections.

But they didn't, of course (and never would in this part of town), which explained why they had to settle for hanging all over Britt and his teammates rather than concerning themselves with their own pathetic lives.

Though they all crowded into the back of the classroom— alongside Steven, who always sat in the back in every class—none of them looked at him. Fine with Steven. They didn't bother him, and he didn't bother them. For the most part. It had been two years since anyone had said anything to Steven about his face. Back then, in junior high, Steven's hormonal changes had made his appearance worse. The counselor had taken the initiative to speak to every English class about Steven's condition and make it clear that anyone who made fun of him would face severe consequences. For a while, the teasing went undercover. And then it simply slept as people matured or found other victims to torture. Short people, fat people, tall people. Really, anyone was fair game.

Steven suspected that as time went on and his face took on another dimension, he'd gone from being a spectacle to a horror. People stayed out of his way not because they were considerate but because the sight of him evoked fear. Jason, Freddie Krueger and Michael Meyers kind of fear.

Steven had begun to settle into this face-imposed isolation. It was comfortable. Easier than trying to fit in. And he'd almost fallen under the impression that he could finish his high school career in peace until the day he saw the note Britt and his crew had been passing around during world history class. Steven watched as one student after another opened the note glanced at its contents and stifled laughter. Normally, he would ignore such childishness, but when Amy Mingersoll passively glanced at Steven and then mouthed to Britt, "You're so mean," Steven knew this note had something to do with him.

Amy balled up the note and set the paper in the empty book bin underneath her chair, obviously refusing to pass it to the next person.

After class, curiosity got the best of Steven. He stalled in his desk for a few moments after the bell rang, then when the coast cleared, he snatched the crumpled paper from under Amy's desk. Quickly, he smoothed the paper against his book cover and flipped it over to view the note. It was a caricature of Steven kissing Amy (depicted by a shirt with her name on it). Of course, Steven's face was grossly amplified to cover Amy's neck and head. Finally, a speech bubble coming from Amy: I can't breathe!

Anger shot through Steven's body. He wondered how anyone could be this stupid. Well, not just anyone. Britt Culverhouse. After all these years of trading and grading papers, Steven knew unmistakably that Britt had created the drawing.

Steven had no intentions of reporting this incident to the principal. He'd handle it his own way.

Alternative school isn't so bad. It starts almost a half hour later than the regular school and we get a longer lunch. No P.E. class, not that I could participate anyway. If I move around too much and get my blood pumping hard, I could turn into a bloody mess.

The best thing about this school is the fact that I have my own cubicle, facing the wall. No one stares at me because, from behind, there's nothing different about me.

When I was a kid, I actually tried to put a brown paper bag over my head. I'd seen people on cartoons do it, so I figured it was okay. I cut out two eye-holes and slipped the grocery sack in place. When my mom saw me, she cried and tried to feed me that age-old cliché every parent with a less-than-perfect child tells their kid: *God made you special.*

I didn't believe her then, and I don't believe her now. This wasn't my idea of "special" and I didn't think it was His, either. I think I'm just something weird that happened in nature – like the platypus. I'm okay with that. I only wish other people could be okay with it, too, and leave me alone.

Now that I'm thinking about it, this alternative school might be the best place for me after all. I just do the assignments the teachers give me and then put my head down on the desk for the rest of the day. Even if I didn't like this place, I'd better get used to it because I've got the rest of the school year plus the first semester of next year to serve my time. I regret putting my mom through a disciplinary conference, and I feel a little bad about messing up Amy's letterman jacket, but Britt deserved it.

I'd do it all over again if I had to.

The whole Valentine's Day hoopla seemed nothing more than a nuisance to Steven; one more reminder that he'd probably never have a girlfriend, never have anyone to buy a teddy bear and a dozen roses for. In fact, when he'd gone to the CVS pharmacy to pick out a box of chocolates for his scheme, he'd been amazed to find how cheap they were. He'd laughed to himself, thinking, "I could have more than one girlfriend at this price." He'd picked up a bottle of red hair dye and a few other things he needed to carry out his plan.

After nearly three hours, Steven had created the perfect payback. He could hardly sleep.

The next day, as soon as the bell rang dismissing second period, Steven rushed to his third period class and stealthily slipped the heart-shaped box from his backpack and placed it on Britt's desk.

Britt and his friends entered the room. It took them a while to make it to the back corner, joking and laughing so loudly the teacher had to give them a warning even though the bell hadn't rung yet.

After what seemed like a hundred years, Britt noticed the box and the note attached. He mocked, "Awww, which one of you guys gave me this?"

His jock friends laughed at him, and one of them said, "Maybe it's from Big Shonda."

Steven winced. Big Shonda, the largest girl in the school, sat pretty high up on the list of outcasts, too.

"Hey, there's a card. Read it," Amy ordered.

Britt obeyed. "To Britt. I love your face. From your secret admirer."

A collective "Ooooh!" flowed from the group.

"Forget that, open it, dawg. I'm hungry," from Renard Jackson.

Steven couldn't have planned it better if he'd paid Renard to set up Britt.

As he watched Britt lift the top off the box, Steven's heart raced. Would it work? Would anyone get hurt?

Then it happened. Spllllat! A burst of red liquid squirted all over Britt's face and sprayed the people standing to his left and right. The other students in the room scattered in fear as profanity flew through the air.

"Aaaargh!" Britt hollered while spitting almost simultaneously. He threw the box to the ground and the last remnants of the hair dye mixed with a bit of glue spilled onto the white tiled floor.

Steven had read online that the glue would actually make the dye adhere to Britt's face longer. Whether or not that was true, he wasn't sure. But it was worth a try.

"Oh my Gaaa! Look at my jacket!" Amy screamed, trying to wipe off the hair dye. She stopped, however, when she realized that she was only making matters worse.

Renard looked down at his shirt and threatened, "I'm gonna kill somebody!"

Just then, the bell rang and Mr. Cantrell walked into the classroom to find the bright red fiasco ensuing. "What's going on here? Is everyone okay?"

"No!" Britt replied. "Look at us!"

"Are you hurt in any way?" the teacher rephrased the question. "No."

"Okay. Stay right here. We'll get to the bottom of this."

When the principal asked me if I'd seen who planted the box, I told him the truth. He thanked me for my honesty and then read through the student handbook, showing me where what I'd done could be classified as a "terrorist act" since I created panic in the classroom. I sat there listening, with my face down because I could tell the principal was uncomfortable looking at me.

Still, I wanted him to know I did it and why. I wanted everyone to know for my sake and for all the Big Shondas, too. Just leave "special" people alone. We've got enough problems as it is.

Even more than that, I wanted Britt to know what it feels like to be stared at everywhere he goes. To see people's faces morph in confusion when they look at him, trying to make sense of what might have happened, hoping it would never happen to them. I wanted Britt to think twice about stopping in the middle of the day to fill up his tank with gas, maybe change his mind and go later, when it's darker outside. I wanted him to understand.

I saw him walking by the portables yesterday. It's not cold out, but he was hiding behind the hood of his jacket. I used to be able to hide the hemangioma but I can't any more. It's gotten too big. It's me, now.

I caught a glimpse of his face under the hoodie. It's still slightly pink. Won't be long now before his skin returns to normal. He's lucky.

After Reading – "Unlucky"

1. Why did Steven choose this type of revenge?
2. Do you think Amy was really trying to protect Steven's feelings or not?
3. How would you feel if people were staring at you all the time?

Writing Prompts

1. Write a paper about the importance of being respectful at all times.
2. Re-write this story from Amy's point of view.

A Different World

Vocabulary Guide – "A Different World"

Words (in order of appearance)	Definition	Example Sentence
Perpetrator	A person who does something illegal or wrong	The perpetrator almost got away with the crime.
Repast	A meal; usually following a special occasion	We brought food to the church for the repast.
Roundabout	Not getting straight to the point; indirect	She asked the question in a roundabout way to avoid upsetting her little sister.
Proposition	Offer or suggest something to be considered	He propositioned the school to see if they would place a crossing guard at the intersection.
Scold	Fuss at someone	My mother scolded me when she saw my report card.
Commotion	Noisy activity	The commotion woke the baby.
Ornate	Covered with many decorations	It took him weeks to create the ornate design in the wood.
Mimic	Copy the way someone speaks or acts	Children often mimic their parents.
Major	Study something as your main subject in college	She majored in biology because she wanted to become a veterinarian

Before Reading – "A Different World"
1. Where do you see yourself ten years from now?
2. How would you describe your neighborhood?
3. How do you handle death?
4. What are some stereotypes about poor people? Rich people? Middle-class people?
5. How do you define "rich"?
6. Do people change when they get an education or training?

You ever heard the saying that sometimes the worst thing to happen to you could also be the best thing? Well, it's true. It happened to me. Two years ago, on Christmas Day, my grandmother, Big, died. She was more like my mother than my grandmother. She got legal custody of me when I was two and raised me until she passed away, when I was sixteen. Big was my heart, and a lot of people said she and I were just alike— serious and quiet.

I can't say I was surprised when she died, though. The doctors told her a long time ago to stop smoking cigarettes, but she didn't listen.

"You've got to die of something," Big would cough. "Might as well be something you like."

Big's house had always been a place where everyone in the family knew they could come and stay if things got bad. My Aunt Rene moved back every time she broke up with whomever she'd been living with. Seemed like every time she came back, she brought another child with her. Rene had four kids by the time Big died.

Every couple of years, my mother would get evicted. Then she'd come and lived with Big, but my mother never stayed for more than a few months because she and Big didn't get along too well. They argued like cats and dogs, mostly about me.

I figured it was wrong to wish my mother would leave, but I couldn't help it. When my mother drank and got high, she got sticky fingers. She stole all the money I'd collected for my school's cookie dough fundraiser when I was in seventh grade.

Big had kicked my mother out again and told her not to come back, but Big didn't mean it. Everyone knew Big's heart.

When my mother needed a place to stay that following year, Big let her move back in again. The cycle continued.

My Uncle Lavon stayed at Big's house when he wasn't in jail. Every time he got out, he'd move back into my bedroom with his girlfriend, Tijuanda, so I'd have to sleep on the couch in the front room.

I hated sleeping in the front room because the only thing standing between me and all the chaos in my neighborhood was a rickety wooden door on Big's 60-year-old house. One time, somebody broke in the house and I had to pretend I was asleep while the thief took the television off the coffee table less than a foot away from my face. I think the perpetrator knew I was awake, but he must have decided not to bother me so long as I didn't bother him.

Anyway, just so happened that when Big died, Uncle Lavon was out of jail. He and Tijuanda started making plans for Big's funeral. Suddenly, Big's house was filled with family members and a few people from a church Big visited every Easter.

In the midst of planning for the funeral, Uncle Lavon said he was calling Uncle Raymond to help pay for Big's final expenses. I really didn't think that was a good idea. I'd only seen Uncle Raymond three times, but I'd heard his name all my life. Big said Raymond was her shining star since he was the only one of her kids who graduated from both high school and college, but everyone else seemed to think Uncle Raymond was wack.

Uncle Lavon said Raymond was a nerd. Aunt Rene said Raymond always thought he was better than everyone else. Back when I was in elementary school, we got an invitation to Uncle Raymond's wedding. My mother ripped it to pieces.

She'd fussed, "Raymond's always looked down on the rest of the family. I wonder if his prissy little wife knows he grew up right here in Brooks Park!"

At that moment, I'd gotten the bright idea to ask my mother why she'd never married my father. She had laughed, "Samayia, you'd better take your nose out of all those books I see you reading. If you get married, you'll lose your housing forever! I bet they don't show you *that* in all those fairy tales, huh?"

My uncle Raymond, his wife Gracie, and their 8-year-old daughter, Kendra, stayed in a hotel when they got to town for the funeral. I should have known they would think they were too good to stay in Brooks Park.

At the funeral, Uncle Raymond hardly even cried. His wife, Gracie, cried more than him.

When we all went to the back of the church for the repast, I had to sit across from Uncle Raymond and Gracie because the organizers wanted all the family to sit together.

"How are you doing in school, Samayia?" Uncle Raymond asked. His deep voice sounded like a radio announcer, and his bald head reminded me of my principal. He looked like he had the kind of job where he was always doling out consequences.

I kept my eyes on my plate. "Good."

"What are your plans after graduation?" Gracie asked.

Since she had actually cried at Big's funeral, I decided to look Gracie in the eyes when I answered. "I don't know, Aunt Gracie, probably get a job."

She smiled and continued, "Just call me Gracie.

"Where do you think you might work?"

"I don't know. Probably at a restaurant or something. Work my way up."

Uncle Raymond interrupted with, "I hear you like to read."

Instinctively, my eyes locked on his. "Who said that?" How dare he act like he knew anything about me.

"Don't shoot me," he laughed. "Big told me that you enjoyed reading. She said your library card looked like it had been in World War III."

"I *used* to like reading. They closed the Brooks Park branch library." I burst his bubble.

"And you let that stop you from reading?" he fussed. "What about your school's library?"

"The books at my school is from 'bout 1985."

Uncle Raymond shook his head. "That's ridiculous. But you should never let other people stop you from getting what you want in life."

I barked, "It ain't my fault they don't have good books in the library. We're in *Brooks Park*, remember?"

Gracie gently laid her hand on Uncle Raymond's wrist. "Samayia, if you'd like to start reading again, I'd love to help."

My heart thumped hard in my chest. "How?"

"I can get you a bookstore gift card and you can order online," she suggested.

"I ain't got no computer." I checked her.

Uncle Raymond asked, "Don't they have them at your school?"

"Yeah, I guess. But I don't have a way to get to the store and pick up the books."

Gracie smiled again. "Don't worry. They'll deliver the books to you."

Uncle Raymond shook his head. "No, that's not gonna work."

"Why not?" I snapped at him.

Calmly, he replied, "Because if a huge brown truck pulls up to Big's house and drops off a package on the doorstep while you're at school, what are the chances that package will still be sitting there by the time you get home?"

He had a point. I sank into my chair and muttered, "Zero."

"I *know* Brooks Park," he said.

"There goes the plan." I sighed.

"Don't give up so easily, my young niece," he started again with the radio voice. "Let's think of plan B. You want the books, but you don't want them delivered to Big's house. What else can you do?"

I shrugged. "I don't know."

He shook his head again. "Anck! Wrong answer. Think. What can you do to get these books despite the fact that you live in Brooks Park?"

"I guess…have 'em sent somewhere else."

"Where?" he probed, squinting his eyes.

I peered back at him. "To someone who doesn't live in Brooks Park."

"Do you know anyone who doesn't live in Brooks Park?" Uncle Raymond quizzed.

"No."

"What about your teachers?" Gracie asked.

I had to look at her like she was crazy. "I don't know my teachers like that."

Uncle Raymond chuckled. "I'll bet your English teacher would love to help."

The next week, I told Mr. Colbert about my situation and asked if he would be willing to have the books delivered to him and then bring them to me at school.

You'd have thought I offered to give him a kidney. "Samayia, that would be wonderful!" he gushed.

When I got home from school, I asked Uncle Lavon if I could use his cell phone to call Uncle Raymond.

He sat on his bed with bloodshot eyes, looking half-drunk while Tijuanda lay motionless behind him, her matted mass of black and blonde hair covering the side of her face entirely. The dark room reeked of marijuana. My first thought was that I had to tell Big about this. She smoked cigarettes, but she didn't allow marijuana in her home.

Then I remembered Big was dead.

"Whatchu need to call Raymond for?" Uncle Lavon questioned me.

"Gracie is going to order books for me online."

Uncle Lavon's ears must have heard music. "Raymond and Gracie giving you money?"

"They're not giving me money. They're just helping me buy books."

"I don't see why they're helping you pay for books when they can't help save Big's house."

His words hit me hard in the stomach. "What?" I managed to stammer.

Uncle Lavon continued, "Big got some kind of reverse mortgage on this house to where after the homeowner is dead, the mortgage company can sell the house. Unless I come up with some money. Fast."

Though her body didn't move, Tijuanda suddenly yelled, "What you sittin' here for, then? Get out there and hustle."

And hustle Uncle Lavon did. Except he didn't hustle *out there.* He started hustling from Big's house. All day and all night, different people came in and out of the house. Or sometimes, they just blew a horn and Uncle Lavon or Tijuanda went out to their car to make a drug transaction.

I moved into Big's old bedroom and locked myself inside most of the time with my wonderful, glorious books—thanks to Gracie and Uncle Raymond.

A few weeks after Big died, Aunt Rene moved back in with her kids, which brought lots of babysitting into my life. Plus, I had to move out of Big's room. The front room was no longer an option for sleeping at night, which only left the kitchen or the bathroom for me.

I opted to retire in the bathroom at night, since it had a lock that I could put between me and Uncle Lavon's "customers." With three adults and five minors, including myself, the bathroom seemed the busiest place in the house—next to the front room, of course. Several times throughout the night, I'd have to get up to let someone use the restroom.

Nights like this, I cried myself to sleep because there was no way on earth Big would have made me bunk on a bathroom floor so Uncle Lavon could disrespect her home by turning it into a crackhouse. If Big could see this, she would hop out of her grave and slap him silly because Big didn't allow illegal activity in her house. "You might live around crime," she'd say, "but crime don't have to live in you."

Even when Aunt Rene moved out again, tears visited me

almost every night.

If it hadn't been for my friend, Alexis, I probably would have been failing out of school. Alexis and I had a lot of the same classes together, so when we got on the bus after school, we'd sit next to each other and rush through our homework during the 25-minute stop-and-go journey.

What you get for number five?" she asked.

"B is greater than fifty-three."

Alexis wrinkled her nose. "I got twenty-seven."

I flipped to the back of the book to check my answer. "Fifty three."

"I should have known. You always have the right answer when the teachers ask questions. You so smart." She heartily erased her markings. "How you come up with fifty-three?"

After I walked Alexis through my steps, she found her error and made the correction on her paper.

We finished the math and then started on social studies. As we entered Brooks Park and the bus driver began making stops, Alexis and I packed our books.

"We'll have to finish this in the morning," I said.

The bus driver stopped at my corner and, suddenly, the bus filled with *ooohs!* and *aaaahs!*

"Somebody got busted!" one of the boys on the bus yelled.

I glanced down the street and realized that the law enforcement hoopla centered on Big's house. Four police cruisers, a big tank truck, and an ambulance littered the lawn.

The normal slew of students got off at my corner, but my behind was frozen in place.

"Young lady," the bus driver accosted me while looking through his rectangular mirror, "you getting off?"

I shook my head. "No."

Quickly, I begged Alexis, "Can I go to your house?"

"Yeah."

Alexis didn't ask any questions. She just turned on the television when we got to her house. I guess the look on my face said I didn't feel much like talking.

When Alexis's mom got home from work, she asked in a roundabout way when I'd be leaving.

"She has to wait for her uncle to come back because she doesn't have her key," Alexis covered for me.

By 7:30, I thought it was probably safe to go back home. However, thanks to the end of daylight saving time, the sky was completely dark. "You can't walk through Brooks Park by yourself at night," Alexis whispered. "Especially not if you plan on taking the shortcut through Berry Hill."

"Do it look like I got a choice?"

"Guess not."

It was bad enough I had to walk through Brooks Park. Berry Hill apartments made my situation ten times worse. Every time the apartment owners tried to illuminate the dark corners of the complex, people shot out the light bulbs.

I grabbed my backpack and took my most valuable possession—a five dollar bill—out of the side compartment. I stuffed the money inside my sock in case somebody jacked me on the way home.

"Don't forget your earrings," Alexis warned.

"They fake."

She crossed her arms. "You think a crackhead gon' care if they fake?"

I followed her lead, removing my cubic zirconium earrings and pushing them deep into my front pocket.

"You got a weapon?" she asked.

I smacked my lips. "I didn't know I was gonna be walking around Brooks Park when I left home this morning, Alexis, otherwise I would."

"Here." She opened her top drawer and then handed me a pocketknife. "It won't kill anybody, but if you get 'em in the eye, that'll stop 'em!" She made stabbing motions in the air.

"Alexis, it ain't that serious." I laughed a little, hoping I was right, yet grasping the knife firmly in my hand.

"Samayia, you gotta be ready for anything in our 'hood." A tinge of sadness laced her voice.

"Well, maybe one day we'll get out of here."

Now it was Alexis's turn to laugh. "Yeah, right. I'll see you in the morning. If you survive."

"Bye, Alexis," I said while shaking my head.

"Peace out."

The cold January wind slapped my face as my feet hit the sidewalk. Quickly, I trekked up Alexis's street and crossed over to Lee Road. If I cut through Berry Hill, I could be home in about seven minutes—versus fifteen minutes if I went around the entire complex.

Big never allowed me to walk through Berry Hill. Yes, I'd done it a few times, but never with her permission. And never at night.

I ducked through the cut-open chain link fence and entered the premises of Berry Hill. Already, I could smell marijuana, and hear a man and a woman arguing.

"Shut up!" someone yelled.

"Come *shut* me up!" came from the man. This, of course, led to a second argument.

I saw one old guy standing up right beside an abandoned children's swing. Asleep. I realized he must be on heroin.

"You looking for something?" a man propositioned me from his window.

"No."

My feet worked double-time to get me through the main courtyard, where two boys struggled to keep their pit bulls from pursuing me. The only thing stopping me from sprinting at that point was the fear that if I ran, the dogs would break free and eat me alive.

With the exit gate in view, my heart calmed a bit. That's when someone sitting on a barbecue grill whistled at me. "Say, lil' momma, you sure walkin' fast. What's your rush?"

I ignored him, keeping my head down.

"Say," he continued, "you got somewhere to go?"

My pace accelerated to a jog.

"Lil' momma, wait up."

I looked back, horrified to find that this man was following me. I took off running.

"Hey!" he called. "Stop her!"

All of a sudden, two women—dressed like they were going to a club—stopped playing a card game and looked my way. I ran faster, my arms pumping so hard I was afraid the knife might slip out of my fist.

"Cookie, get up and stop her!" the man ordered.

I had a good twenty-foot head start on Cookie, but I looked over my shoulder and she caught up with me in no time. She lunged toward me, grabbing my backpack and growling, "You heard Papa talkin' to you!"

My body jerked when she grabbed my backpack, but somehow I managed to wiggle my arms out of the straps and get ahead of her again. Something inside me said, *Don't look back*, so this time, I didn't.

To this day, I don't remember anything that happened from the moment Cookie snatched my backpack off to the second I closed Big's front door behind me. I must have blacked out from the adrenaline rush.

I stood with my forehead pressed against the door, my eyes surveying the street through the peephole. I had no idea what I'd do if Cookie or Papa had followed me home. Three minutes passed. Five. No Cookie or Papa.

My heart returned to its normal pace, but the silence in Big's house screamed, *You're all alone in this world now!*

No doubt Uncle Lavon and Tijuanda would probably be gone for a long time, especially considering his previous offenses. Last I heard, my mother was staying in Crescent Villas—a step down from Berry Hill. I wouldn't dare move in with Aunt Rene and whatever crazy man she was living with at the moment.

My insides ached as questions bombarded me: *What am I going to do now? How am I going to pay the bills and eat? What about the reverse mortgage?* I thought about calling Uncle Raymond, but what could he do? Besides, he was mean and stuck-up.

If only Big was alive, this wouldn't be happening to me. I'd be happy. Safe. And there would be someone on the planet who actually loved and cared about me.

I trudged to Big's bedroom and stood in front of her closet. She didn't have many clothes—maybe five shirts, a few pairs of pants, a house coat, and a dress she wore for special occasions. I needed to smell Big's scent again. I opened my arms wide and encircled all the clothes in Big's closet. Then I smushed them all together in a tight hug. I closed my eyes and took a deep breath. The smell of Big rushed through my nostrils and, for a moment, I suspended reality and imagined myself hugging Big. I could almost hear her whisper in my ear, "Everything's gon' be alright, Samayia."

The next audible words I heard were, "Stop. Put your hands up where I can see them."

Apparently, the cops had been watching Big's house even after they arrested Uncle Lavon. I think the officer believed me when I told him that my grandmother had recently died and that I had nothing to do with Uncle Lavon. But because I was sixteen and had no guardian, he called Child Protective Services (CPS). I packed up a few clothes and a CPS case worker, Mrs. Gonzalez, carted me off to some kind of clinic-looking building, where she later asked me if there was anyone in my family I could stay with.

"No, not really." I shook my head and looked through a crack in the doorway. I could see several girls sitting on sofas in a large living area watching television. Their expressionless faces reminded me of the way Uncle Lavon looked when Big took me to see him in jail. He was just biding his time, bored to death, he'd said.

"Ten o'clock. Lights out!" A heavyset woman with a long spiral ponytail waltzed into their room and turned off the television.

The girls moaned collectively. "Oh, come on! Stop treating us like babies!"

"Should have thought about that before you got yourself put in here," the woman scolded.

Mrs. Gonzalez closed the door, regaining my attention. "Where is your father?"

"Dead. To me, at least."

She scribbled something on her notepad. "Your mother?"

"My grandmother had custody of me, but she passed last month."

"I see." Her lips pursed in sympathy. "Well, until we can find a suitable environment for you, you'll have to stay here."

Suddenly, a loud ruckus came from the room just beyond Mrs. Gonzalez' door.

"You idiot!" was followed by a string of curse words and name-calling. That place was a zoo, and after my experience running through Berry Hill, I knew I couldn't survive there.

Mrs. Gonzalez kept talking, as though she didn't hear the commotion. "What school do you attend?"

"Maybe there is somebody I can stay with," I interrupted her line of questioning. "My Uncle Raymond."

Three hours later, at almost one o'clock in the morning, Uncle Raymond and Gracie picked me up from the group home. I know it's crazy, but the first thing that hit me when we got into his Range Rover was how the genuine leather smelled like rich people.

"You hungry?" Uncle Raymond asked as he pulled out of the parking lot.

"Yes."

Gracie suggested, "Wendy's is open all night."

"That's fine."

Gracie tried to make small talk with me, but I wasn't in the mood.

We stopped and got food, and then Uncle Raymond drove to a hotel for the night.

I'd never been inside a hotel before—only read about them in books. The books didn't do hotels justice. The lobby area reminded me of the movie *Titanic*, with its ornate decorations and gold-framed paintings lining the walls. Thick marble columns anchored a grand staircase; the kind where rich girls stood on the top step, posing for their wedding pictures in fancy white gowns that probably cost more than Big's whole house.

Our hotel room had both a master suite and a living room, divided by French doors. We had our own small kitchen, too, with a refrigerator, a microwave, and a cooking range.

My bathroom already had soap, shampoo, and lotion on the counter. I thought, *I could live here forever.*

The next morning, Gracie woke me up and asked if I wanted to order any breakfast from room service.

"What's room service?"

She explained, "It's when they bring the food to your room."

"Yeah. I guess."

I took a look at the menu and wondered how on earth three pancakes and two slices of bacon could cost ten dollars. "This is too expensive," I told Gracie, slamming the menu shut.

"Don't worry about how much it costs. Just get what you'd like to eat for breakfast." She winked at me.

Never before had it occurred to me that some people just buy what they need without thinking about how much it costs first. When Big and I went to the grocery store, we always looked at the price of everything before we decided what to throw in the shopping cart because we couldn't exceed the amount of money credited to her LoneStar card at the beginning of the month.

As it turns out, that breakfast was only the beginning of things I'd learn while living with Uncle Raymond. For starters, their neighborhood was clean. I think a whole week passed before I saw even a plastic grocery sack drifting down the street. And people were friendly. Kids rode their bikes outside; people walked their dogs and said "Hello" as they passed.

Uncle Raymond's house had four bedrooms and a pool in the back yard. I stayed in a room upstairs, adjacent to Kendra. We shared a bathroom. I quickly realized that she looked up to me. "Samayia, can you do my hair like yours?" she'd ask almost every other day.

Even though I enjoyed Kendra's company, Gracie and Uncle Raymond always offered to take Kendra somewhere if they were going out at night. "Kendra isn't your responsibility," Gracie said. "We didn't bring you here to be a live-in babysitter."

I wished Aunt Rene shared the same philosophy.

My new school, Stanley Creek High, was another big surprise. All the stalls in the bathrooms had doors that actually closed. Plus, all the toilets worked and there was soap in the dispenser. Every once in a while, I saw where someone had written something on a wall, but the next day, the graffiti would be gone.

I'd heard some kids got suspended for smoking. Drugs are everywhere, I suppose, but people at Stanley Creek didn't talk about smoking weed as though it was just like eating candy.

My teachers didn't think I was so smart at my new school, though. Compared to the kids at Stanley Creek, I guess I was average. My classmates raised their hands and answered questions correctly as often as I did. At first, I thought maybe the teachers at Brooks Park High had been kidding me. Maybe I wasn't so smart after all. But when I took my first test in Algebra II, I got a 93.

Uncle Raymond said that just proved I could do anything I put my mind to. "You thought about what college you want to attend?" he asked me as we devoured another one of Gracie's homemade dishes.

I replied, "I don't know. College costs a lot of money, right?"

He nodded. "Yeah, but you're broke, right?"

"Yeah."

"That's the best thing about college in this country. Kids from neighborhoods like Brooks Park qualify for all kinds of scholarships and grants. You won't have to pay a penny to go to college. I didn't," he declared.

"We could go online tonight and start looking at colleges if you'd like," Gracie advised.

Kendra exclaimed, "Can I look for a college, too?"

Later that night, after Gracie and I had finished researching colleges, I lay in my cushy bed thinking about my past and my future. Every kindergartner in Brooks Park said they wanted to be a doctor or a lawyer. By the time we made it to middle school, however, only of few of us still liked school. High school only brought more disappointments—people dropping out, getting killed, going to jail, getting pregnant. Not *everyone* in Brooks Park did these things, of course. Just seemed like it sometimes.

Until I talked to my uncle, I hadn't given college a serious thought. Now, it looked as though I might actually get to fulfill every little kid's dream of doing something important with my life.

Uncle Raymond had made arrangements, through CPS and the police, to allow me to gather the last of my belongings and a few pictures of Big before the house was sold.

I listened to Uncle Raymond talk most of the three-hour drive back to Brooks Park. He told me the same things teachers, principals, and Big told me in the past, but now it all made sense coming from someone who was living the kind of life I wanted to lead. I longed to be able to walk in a store and get what I wanted, drive where I needed to go instead of waiting for a bus, and live in a neighborhood where gunshots weren't background noise.

Most of all, if I ever got married and had kids, I wanted them to grow up like Kendra. That girl had it made and she didn't even know it.

When we reached Big's house, I rushed inside hoping to feel an inkling of Big's presence. There was nothing left. Not even the sense that I'd lived in the house. Everything looked different. Tattered. Worn.

I took a deep breath, then went back to my old bedroom where I packed up the rest of my shoes, clothes, and novels. Then I went to Big's room and grabbed a photo of the two of us blowing out the candles on her last birthday cake. My heart ached inside my chest again. I was thankful for all the new opportunities I'd learned about since living with Uncle Raymond and Gracie, but I still wished more than anything that Big would come walking into the room and say, "Samayia, put your stuff away, baby, I'm back now. You can come home."

Tears came so quickly I could barely see the way back to

the SUV.

"You alright?" Uncle Raymond asked as he met me on the sidewalk.

"No," I squealed.

Uncle Raymond pulled me into a tight embrace and let me cry all over his Polo shirt. "It's alright, Samayia," he comforted me. "Everything's gonna be alright."

"But I miss her," I cried.

"I do, too," he admitted.

"You *do*?" I looked up at him and noticed the pool of water forming in his eyes.

"Of course I do," he said. "She *was* my mother."

We stood outside for a little longer, then Uncle Raymond said it was time we left.

I strapped myself into the front seat and suddenly remembered Alexis's knife, which I'd throw in my purse during this last visit to Big's house. "Uncle Raymond, can you take me to my friend's house? I need to return something to her."

He agreed and I directed him to Alexis's house. Her mother answered the door, took one look at Uncle Raymond's Range Rover, and questioned, "You dealin' drugs now?"

"No. That's my uncle's car."

"What kinda job he got?" she wanted to know.

"He's a therapist."

"He married?"

"Yes, ma'am."

She rolled her eyes, then she told me I could go into Alexis's room.

"Hey!" Alexis greeted me with open arms. "How you been?"

"I'm good. You?"

She smacked her lips. "I'm failing Algebra because you ain't here to help me."

"Anyway," I sang. "You're perfectly capable of succeeding without me."

"Snap." She tucked in her chin. "What's with all the big words?"

"What?"

Alexis mimicked me in a chirpy voice, "...perfectly capable of succeeding without me."

I pulled some slang to let her know I was still the same old Samayia. "Don't trip, aiiight?"

"*That's* my girl. But for real, Samayia, you gotta do something about those clothes."

I glanced down at my khaki pants and white, collared shirt. "We wear uniforms at my new school."

"Dang." She shook her head. "That's wack. But check it, I've got some stuff you might like. Close my door."

I obeyed her order, wondering what mischief she was hiding from her mother. Alexis quietly opened her closet door and displayed what must have been thousands of dollars worth of clothes and handbags. "Oh my gosh, Alexis, where did you get all this?"

"Shhhh!" she whispered.

Upon closer examination of the items in her closet, I recognized several name brands from Gracie's wardrobe— Coach, Donna Karen, Calvin Klein, Tommy Hilfiger. I stood in amazement, my mouth almost touching the floor.

Alexis winked at me. "Me and my cousin Trey got a plan. We gon' be rich!"

A few seconds later, all the pieces came together in my mind. The merchandise, the brands, her secrecy. I whispered the obvious. "Alexis, you're stealing this stuff?"

"Duh!"

She put her index finger on my forehead.

"I steal it, then Trey takes it to the barber shops and the bazaar and sells it. He gives me half the money. Last week, we made like seven hundred dollars."

"But, Alexis…you're a booster."

"It ain't your stuff," she defended herself. "What do you care?"

"You're gonna get caught. Then what? I mean, think about the consequences."

She wagged her head. "I'm sixteen. Ain't nothin' much they can do to me right now, plus it'll come off my record when I'm twenty-one. Besides, I ain't gon' get caught. You sound like my Momma."

I racked my brain for a way to stuff two months worth of Uncle Raymond's lectures into a two-minute conversation with Alexis. "Look, you have to think about your future. You're smart. You've got your whole life ahead of you, Alexis. Did you know you can go to college for free?"

She crossed her arms. "I ain't goin' to school for no four more years."

"What about that dental assistant school you wanted to go to?"

She brushed me off. "My cousin Diondra went to one of those schools, but it was too hard. She dropped out and she had to pay all that money back. Now she won't even get her income tax money for, like, the next two years."

I sighed. "Alexis, you're better than this." Then I used Big's words, "You might live in Brooks Park, but Brooks Park doesn't have to live in you."

Alexis slammed her closet door shut. "You been out of the 'hood two months, and you already actin' bourgie. Come in here usin' all these big words and tryin' to tell me what I need to do. If you didn't have that uncle of yours, you'd be boostin' right along with me. So just get out of here!"

I set her knife on the dresser. "I came to give this back to you."

"Yeah, you prob'ly don't need knives where you live now."

I walked toward the door and grabbed the door knob. I pleaded one more time before leaving. "Alexis, please stop boosting. You're going to ruin your life."

She grabbed the knife. "I said get out."

That was my last visit to Brooks Park. Almost two years ago. Yes, I still miss Big like crazy, but I know she wouldn't want me to stay in Brooks Park if I had another option. I've decided I won't go back until I have something to give.

Today, I'm a freshman in college, thanks to a second chance. I spent a year in job corps earning my cosmetology certificate, then I went to college. I'm majoring in psychology, like my uncle. Hopefully, someday, I'll be able to get inside someone's head the way he got inside mine and make a difference. I'll set up an office right in the middle of Brooks Park so I can talk to kids. The first thing I'll say is: don't let anyone look down on you because you grew up in a tough neighborhood. Secondly, I'll let them know there's another world beyond Brooks Park. A totally different world.

After Reading – "A Different World"

1. How did Samayia change after staying with Uncle Raymond for two months?
2. Do you think Samayia and Alexis could or should be friends again?
3. Do you think Samayia's opinion of Uncle Raymond changed after she cried on his shoulder?
4. Alexis said Samayia would have been a booster if it hadn't been for Uncle Raymond. Do you agree or disagree?

Writing Prompts

1. Write an essay about a time when something you thought was bad turned out to be good.
2. Write an essay about the importance of giving back to your community.
3. Write Samayia's first speech to youth in Brooks Park following her college graduation.

It Happened on a Friday

Vocabulary Guide – "It Happened on a Friday"

Words (in order of appearance)	Definition	Example Sentence
Rival	People or groups competing for the same goal	When it came to winning Jasmine's heart, Juan and Carlos were rivals.
Invincible	Unable to be defeated	The army was invincible.
Formidable	Powerfully frightening	The six foot tall, muscular wrestler was a formidable opponent.
Rummage	Search through by moving items around and looking through contents	I rummaged through the silverware drawer to find a spoon.
Lament	Feel sadness or regret	Daniel lamented after being kicked off the team.
Vixen	A well-developed, seductive, sexy woman	My mother says she will not let me leave the house looking like a vixen.
Cinch	Gathered in	Beth cinched her dress with a belt to make herself look thinner.
Audacity	Boldness or daring without thinking about others	Alana had the audacity to curse at her grandparents.
Forthright	Being completely open and honest	Sheila's parents wished she would be more forthright about her friends.
Summon	Call for someone to be present	Cory was summoned to court because he witnessed the crime.
Dwell	To focus your attention on something for a long time	Oscar tried not to dwell on the fact that he failed the test.
Protocol	Rules for correct conduct	Protocol requires that all students are required to wear uniforms.

Before Reading – It Happened on a Friday

1. Should children should take care of their parents when their parents get old?
2. Should girls who wear tight, revealing clothes should expect to be treated with disrespect?
3. Do you think that people who have been convicted of crimes against children should not be allowed to live near elementary schools?

Jacob could hardly sleep on Thursday nights because Football Fridays were crazy at Northway High School, and this Friday was the craziest of all. They were playing South High School, their cross-town rivals who also happened to be the defending state champions. Since there was no game last week, Jacob was so pumped that he even dreamed about football the night before. As a defensive end, he always had to be on point.

No one lined up across from Jacob Caldon without feeling the pain. He was six feet, 250 pounds of pure defense. He was invincible and untouchable. He was, after all, Jacob Caldon – co-captain of the football team that was about to put Northway back on the map.

The irony in all of this, however, was that no one in Jacob's small family seemed to notice his importance. "Jacob, make sure Rebecca gets to school on time," his mother would warn as she walked out the door. In addition to making sure that he walked his little sister to school, Jacob had a million chores to complete around the house. He was responsible for the trash, the yard, the dog, and often cooking the food.

This was because his Mom was single and worked full-time as an administrative assistant while going to school part-time to earn a degree. Jacob could flatten the most formidable opponent, but one word from his Mom could make Jacob feel one inch tall. Jacob was a good son, and he looked forward to the day he could sign a fat football contract and take care of his mother financially since his father hadn't been man enough to do the job.

Stephanie rummaged through the pile of laundry on the couch to no avail. Nothing but socks, towels, and undergarments. Despite their mother's warnings, Stephanie's older sister, Ashley, never kept up with the laundry. Once again, Stephanie had no clean clothes to wear to school. But with her mother already gone to work and Ashley gone to drill team practice, Stephanie didn't have anyone to listen to her complaints.

Stephanie walked from the living room to her sister's bedroom and pushed back the closet door. Ashley, a senior, was a drama queen/fashion goddess/girly girl. All Ashley seemed to talk about was drill team, friendship problems, and boys. Stephanie, on the other hand, was a studious sophomore who had skipped the third grade and was already well on her way to earning a full scholarship to Texas A&M, where she would study psychology and figure out what the heck was wrong with people like Ashley.

Reluctantly, Stephanie stuffed herself into a pair of her sister's jeans. She zipped them up and quickly swiveled around to get a view of her backside in the mirror atop Ashley's dresser. "Ugh!" Stephanie sighed and fussed to herself. "I could have just painted these things on my body."

The jeans fit so tightly that Stephanie could hardly breathe. And the way her behind stuck out in the back was almost disgusting. "I've got to lose weight," Stephanie lamented, silently vowing to skip dessert over the weekend. She knew, however, that it wouldn't do any good. She had been cursed with her mother's body, which she tried to hide with baggy pants and oversized shirts.

Most girls would have killed to walk a mile in Stephanie's body and hear all the "Oohs!" and "Dangs!" that followed a girl with a perfect silhouette. Even Ashley was jealous of

Stephanie's body and often voiced her belief that God had wasted His talents by giving that body to her little sister.

"If it was me, I'd flaunt it 'til the day I die," Ashley had said more than once.

Stephanie would usually reply, "If it was you, you would have ruined it already."

That was mean, but it was true. Ashley ate like a pig and never exercised, not to mention the way she disrespected her body by wearing hoochie clothes like the very jeans Stephanie was forced to wear that Friday morning.

Stephanie searched through Ashley's closet again for a decent shirt to cover up the curves which made her look like some kind of music video vixen. After several minutes, she gave up. There just wasn't a shirt in Ashley's closet that didn't push dress-code. Stephanie quickly rushed back to her own room, found the least dirty shirt in the hamper, and pulled it over her head. In an instant, Stephanie gathered her hair back into a ponytail, dabbed Vaseline on her lips, slid on a pair of shoes, and headed out the door.

Stephanie met up with her neighbor, Johnna Miles, and they walked to the bus stop together.

"What's on your shirt?" Johnna asked.

"Where?"

"Here – on the back," Johnna said as she pulled up the bottom of Stephanie's shirt.

Stephanie managed to see the bright green spot that Johnna had pointed out. "I can't stand my sister! She didn't wash the clothes, and I had to find the only shirt that didn't smell. But it's got a stain on it!"

Johnna laughed. "Well, at least it's at the bottom. Just tuck it in."

"Easier said than done," Stephanie said under her breath.

When she reached the campus, Stephanie rushed into the restroom. She tried tying a knot on the side of the shirt. She tried folding it up. She even tried turning it inside out, but nothing worked. Stephanie would have to tuck the shirt in or else go around looking like a dirty bum all day. "This is just great," Stephanie said as she unzipped the too-tight jeans to add another layer of definition to her frame. She stood in the mirror and checked herself out again. It was bad – really bad.

Jacob and a few of his teammates – Camron, Isaias, and Kendrick – always met up near the band hall before school. It was a great place to girl-watch. Jacob was standing against the wall exchanging old "yo Momma" jokes with Kendrick when Camron gave Jacob a sharp jab in the ribs. Jacob looked at Camron, whose eyes were focused on an object to the left. Quickly, Jacob followed Camron's line of sight, landing on a perfect Coke-bottle shape. Seriously, her body was like *Kadow!*

"Dang!" Isaias could barely contain himself.

"Who is that?" Camron asked.

As she neared them, Jacob noticed her face. She was pretty, with long black hair and lips that seemed to speak to him: *"Hello, Jacob."* Or was it just his imagination?

The side view was even more heavenly. The way this girl's waist cinched in was unbelievable. He had only seen bodies like this dancing next to Lil' Wayne on stage. Jacob wondered where this girl had been all his life. Seriously, he thought he had seen everyone at school. More importantly, why hadn't *she* seen *him*? He was, after all, Jacob Caldon, and he knew that every girl in school, regardless of race, background, or economic status, wanted to be with him.

"That's an umbrella, ella, ella behind," Kendrick said.

"That ain't real," Camron finally decided as the mystery girl walked past them.

"Yes, it is," Jacob said.

Camron challenged him, "Bet."

"What? You think she's got some implants?" Jacob asked.

"She's got somethin' 'cause it is biologically and mathematically impossible to be that fine in this present world," Camron joked.

"I say it's real," Kendrick agreed.

Jacob suggested, "I say we find out." Slowly, Jacob pulled his back from the wall and, in a moment's time, the four friends followed the girl, laughing and building up nerve all the while.

As Stephanie rounded the corner to get to her class, she suddenly felt someone grab her behind and squeeze it. She stopped in her tracks and spun back around the corner to see who had the audacity to touch her. The boys were running away, so she didn't see their faces. But she did hear the boy wearing the number 76 yell, "It's real, fool!" as he slapped hands with number 29.

Miss McCall was trying her best to teach polynomials, but no one was listening.

"Miss McCall," the vice principal's voice interrupted the wannabe lesson.

"Yes."

"Could you please send Jacob Caldon to the office?"

Jacob stood and announced, "I'm out."

He moseyed into the main entrance area and stuck his head into the office of Mrs. Holloway, Vice Principal Kerry's secretary. "Jacob, have a seat outside. Mr. Kerry will be with you shortly."

Jacob plopped himself down on one of the seats. He hadn't really given much thought to why he was in the office. Jacob was a pretty good student who didn't get in any serious trouble – at least nothing detention couldn't handle.

Then, Jacob saw Kendrick enter the office. "Hey, what are you in for?" Jacob asked.

Kendrick shrugged. "I don't know. What about you?"

Mrs. Holloway broke into their conversation. "Kendrick, Mr. Kerry will see you now."

Jacob waited quietly, and after five minutes, Mr. Kerry came out to escort Jacob to the interior office, where Mrs. Richards, the building principal, was waiting. Mr. Kerry and Mrs. Richards sat across from Jacob with stern expressions.

Mr. Kerry began, "Jacob, I received a report this morning that you sexually assaulted a young lady in the hallway."

Jacob snarled his face in disbelief. "What?"

"Sexual harassment and sexual assault are serious infractions. I want you to know that we take this report seriously and that you need to be very forthright in this discussion," Mrs. Richards advised.

"I haven't done anything. Who said I assaulted somebody?" Jacob wondered aloud.

"Did you ... touch anyone this morning?" Mr. Kerry asked.

Suddenly, Jacob remembered. He remembered that fine girl in the hallway, the one with the umbrella bottom stuffed into those revealing jeans. He didn't even know her name. Come to think of it, she probably didn't know his name, either. That must be why they had called in Kendrick.

They didn't have any proof. It was her word against theirs, and there was no way Jacob was going to confess to something they couldn't prove – especially not today. He couldn't afford to get in any trouble today, not with the biggest game of the season coming up in just a matter of hours.

"I didn't do anything to anybody," Jacob said.

"So, you're saying that you did not touch anyone this morning?" Mrs. Richards asked

"No," Jacob said.

"No, you didn't touch anyone, or no, that's not what you're saying?"

Jacob lied, "I'm saying I didn't touch anybody."

Then he observed Mrs. Richards making notes on a pad of paper, and Jacob realized he needed to leave himself some room for interpretation. "I mean, if I touched somebody ... like on accident ... I ... I just know I didn't assault anybody. I mean, I have a lot of homegirls and stuff."

Mr. Kerry was looking down now, rolling his lips between his teeth, and Jacob knew that it was time to stop talking.

"Can I go back to class now?" Jacob asked.

Mrs. Richards jotted down a few more notes, and then, without another word, she filled out a pass for Jacob to return to class. Jacob stopped off at the restroom to compose himself. He had to stay calm and remember: it was some skank's word against his.

When the sophomores were dismissed to go in the pep rally,

Stephanie begged Mrs. Davis to let her stay in the computer lab so that she could work on an important paper. "I wish all my students were as conscientious as you are, Stephanie," Mrs. Davis said. With that, Mrs. Davis left the room and allowed Stephanie some time alone on the computer. Stephanie quickly opened a blank page and began to document everything that happened on Friday morning, just as Mrs. Richards had commanded her to do.

"Stephanie," Mrs. Richards had said, "if we find out that you made this story up, there will be consequences." According to Mrs. Richards, number 76 denied touching Stephanie's behind.

"Can't you pull the videotape or something?" Stephanie defended herself.

Mrs. Richards nodded, "Only if I have just cause. Can you write up a description of what happened and get it to me by the end of the day?"

Stephanie agreed to write follow-up documentation before 3:30. But as she watched her words fill the empty screen, Stephanie had second thoughts about the whole thing. She had to admit that her day had started off badly, and that the hallway incident was simply the straw that broke the camel's back. When she went to the principal's office to report that number 76 on the football team had groped her behind, Stephanie hoped that the principal would give the boy detention so that he would think twice about touching another girl's body.

But when Mrs. Richards summoned Stephanie back into the office to double-check the story after the boy denied it, Stephanie could tell that this was more serious than she'd imagined. Mrs. Richards called it a "sexual assault."

Now, as Stephanie finished her written account of the incident and printed it, she regretted everything about this Friday. But Stephanie couldn't dwell on that now. Somebody was going down, and it wasn't going to be her. She might regret the way she'd handled things, but the fact still remained: the boy had no right to put his hands on her. Stephanie resolved to do what she had to do. If the law defined what happened as a sexual assault, so be it. Stephanie didn't write the laws. She only wrote the facts.

Friday night's game was a bust. Jacob wasn't in his zone. He missed three key tackles, enabling South to take the lead early in the first quarter. South was up 14-0 at halftime, and things got worse from there. When the smoke cleared, South won 21-10, and the bus ride home was excruciating. Once again, Northway had been defeated. Jacob knew that there was no "I" in team, but he couldn't help thinking the loss was his fault. If only he hadn't been focused on the problem with that girl.

Jacob knew immediately that something was different when he walked toward his second period class Monday morning. Mr. Meyerhaul, Jacob's science teacher, met Jacob at the doorway and instructed him to go to the office.

"Let me just put my stuff down," Jacob said.

Mr. Meyerhaul stopped him. "No, Jacob, I think you ought to take your things with you."

Jacob wondered how much worse his life could get. They lost to South, he was accused of sexual assault, and now he was going back to the office to lie again. He had to lie. Otherwise, he might get suspended, which would mean he couldn't play football, which would mean that he would never be able to buy his Mom her dream house.

In an instant, Jacob's life went from bad to worse. The very woman on his mind – his mother – was sitting in the office with bloodshot eyes.

"Mom?"

Miss Caldon couldn't look at Jacob directly. She looked toward the ground and barely managed to whisper, "I can't believe you've done this to me."

"Mom, it's just a …," Jacob's voice trailed off as he searched for the right words.

"They're calling it an assault, Jacob."

Jacob sat down next to his mother and buried his face in his hands. He could not have imagined this scene in his worst nightmare.

Miss Caldon struggled to keep her voice down. "I saw the tape, Jacob. I cannot believe you would do something like this. I raised you to have respect for women. How would you like it if someone grabbed Rebecca's behind the way you grabbed that girl's?"

Busted.

Jacob confessed, "It was a joke, okay? Camron said –"

"Do you see Camron here right now?" Miss Caldon cut him off. "I don't see anyone here except *you* right now."

Mrs. Holloway motioned for Jacob and Miss Caldon to come to the inner office. Once inside, Jacob nearly fainted. There was Mr. Kelly, Mrs. Richards, and Officer Williams waiting to speak to Jacob and his mother. Everyone was seated, and, finally, Officer Williams spoke. "Before we say anything, I need to advise you and your mother of your rights. Anything you say can and will be used against you, and you don't have to say anything without an attorney present."

"What is this?" Miss Caldon interrupted. "Is...is my son being charged with a crime?"

Right or wrong, Jacob was glad to know that his Mom was on his side.

"Miss Caldon," Mrs. Richards informed Jacob's mother, "as I told you earlier, Jacob denied having groped the young lady's behind. So, I had the young lady write up the incident, which gave me just cause for reviewing the videotape. And any time we have to access videotape, we are required to document the reason and, as a matter of protocol, we are required to notify our campus officers."

"Okay, so what's next?" Miss Caldon asked.

Mr. Kelly proceeded, "Well, the bigger problem with this situation is that Jacob is seventeen, and the young lady he touched is fourteen years old."

"She's fourteen?" Jacob asked in disbelief.

Mr. Kelly nodded and continued, "Because of the age difference, Jacob is classified as an adult, and the victim is classified as a child."

Miss Caldon was confused. "So, what are you saying?"

"We're saying that if we can prove that Jacob touched her inappropriately, he may be charged with fondling a child or indecency with a minor."

"That's ridiculous!" Jacob yelled.

"Wait a minute," Miss Caldon said, hardly able to process the emotions flowing through her body. "Isn't this something the school can handle with *school* consequences?"

"I'm afraid not, Miss Caldon," Mrs. Richards replied. "This is out of our hands at this point. It's the State versus

Jacob, now."

Miss Caldon rose to her feet and declared, "We're not saying another word without a lawyer."

Eleven months later...

Jacob finished packing the last box and said goodbye to his bedroom for the last time. He joined his mother and younger sister at the car and stuffed the final cardboard box into the back seat.

"I don't want to move, Mommy," Rebecca whined again.

Miss Caldon rubbed Rebecca's back for a moment. "I know, Sweetie, but we have to."

Jacob couldn't bear to witness this exchange. It was all his fault. It was bad enough his mother had to spend her hard-earned money on the only attorney they could afford. Jacob pleaded guilty and avoided serving time, but he had to undergo expensive counseling. He was not allowed to return to Northway High School.

Rather than endure the embarrassment of going to an alternative school and trying to explain to football scouts why he wasn't playing any more, Jacob quietly dropped out of school and took the GED exam. After all he had been through, he was thankful to be a free man. But, as a condition of his plea, Jacob had to register as a sex offender, which meant he would no longer be able to live within two thousand feet of a school. Hence, the reason for the family's abrupt move.

As Jacob snapped his seatbelt, the tears flowed from his eyes. He had given up on acting macho several months ago when Miss Caldon told him that she would have to quit going to school and get a second job in order to pay for his attorney.

Since then, Jacob had cried more days than he cared to remember.

As they pulled out of the driveway, Jacob shed yet another tear. He could only hope that this move would signify a new beginning for him, and he could only pray that the fateful Friday would not haunt him forever.

Stephanie packed the last of her belongings and settled them into her father's car. She couldn't believe how much her life had changed in the past eleven months. Once people found out that she was the reason Jacob Caldon was kicked out of school, they never let her forget it. From the time she got on the bus until the time she got home from school, Stephanie was constantly harassed about being a snitch, a goody-two-shoes, and making the entire football team lose focus. She had even received notes in her locker threatening to beat her up and give her something to complain about "for real."

When she could take the harassment no more, Stephanie made a call to her father. Though she hated to move five hundred miles from her Mom, Stephanie had to escape the madness of Northway High School and start a new life. She, too, wanted to leave the past in the past.

After Reading – "It Happened on a Friday"
1. Do you think Jacob deserved what happened to him? Why or why not?
2. Did Stephanie do anything wrong?
3. Could Jacob have avoided a lot of trouble if he'd told the truth when they first asked him about touching Stephanie?
4. Why do you think Stephanie got so angry when Jacob touched her?
5. Would you want to be friends with Stephanie? Jacob?

Writing Prompts
1. Research and write a report on little-known laws affecting teens in your state.
2. Write a letter to the judge who might hear Jacob's appeal letting the judge know whether or not Jacob's sentence should stand.

Secondary Teachers: If you think your students would like these stories, be sure to subscribe to www.WeGottaRead.com, where the author hosts 50 more selections along with ancillary materials. **Students,** be sure to tell your teachers about the website!

About the Author

In addition to her work in the field of education, Michelle ministers through writing and public speaking. Her works include the highly acclaimed *Boaz Brown, Divas of Damascus Road* (National Bestseller), *Falling Into Grace,* which has been optioned for a movie of the week, and the award-winning, bestselling Mama B series. She has published several short stories for high school students through her educational publishing company, Right Track Academic Support Services, at www.WeGottaRead.com.

Michelle regularly speaks at special events and writing workshops sponsored churches, schools, book clubs, and educational organizations.

The Stimpsons are the proud parents of two young adults and one crazy dog.

Visit Michelle online at www.MichelleStimpson.com.

Made in the USA
San Bernardino, CA
11 November 2019